D0467574

The Mark of Conte

THE MARK OF CONTE

SONIA LEVITIN

Collier Books
Macmillan Publishing Company
New York

Collier Macmillan Publishers
London

Collier Books
Macmillan Publishing Company
866 Third Avenue, New York, NY 10022
Collier Macmillan Canada, Inc.

Printed in the United States of America

A hardcover edition of *The Mark of Conte* is available from
Atheneum Publishers, Macmillan Publishing Company.

10 9 8 7 6 5 4 3 2 1

Library of Congress Cataloging-in-Publication Data

Levitin, Sonia, 1934–
The mark of Conte.

Summary: When he realized that the computer at his new
school thinks that he's two people, Conte decides to take a
double course load and graduate in half the time.
[1. High schools—Fiction.   2. Schools—Fiction.
3. Humorous stories]   I. Title.
PZ7.L58Mar   1987   [Fic]   87-1091
ISBN 0-02-044191-6 (pbk.)

Especially for Dan, with love

Contents

The Mark of
Conte

1 The Birth of a Great Idea

Great ideas don't just appear in a single stroke. No. They nestle and settle in the mind, growing layer by layer. Then one day there comes a final cause to make the Great Idea explode in all its brilliance. That's how it was for Conte Mark.

It happened while Conte was walking home from the Freshman Orientation Meeting. The germ of the idea grew quickly, fed by his surging anger. He was angry at that character, Kurt Zelinkowitz. He was mad at the Comminger Catalogue Company, at the high school counselor, and maddest of all at Kirkland Corporation. K.C., as they called it at home, had simply given his father notice last May. He wasn't needed anymore. So they had had to get out of Texas, pack up and move to the town of Vista Mar in California.

Conte had been led to expect great things in California. In glowing terms the realtor had described the town and especially Vista Mar High. But this morning Conte had seen enough to shatter all his illusions. The place stunk.

"Please explain," Conte's dad would have said in his patient, professional manner. "What exactly do you mean, 'stunk'?"

Conte meant that the place was phony clear through. Take the buildings themselves. They'd driven past the school several times, and Conte's parents had admired the wide lawns, the low, Spanish style walls covered with flowering vines.

"Beautiful," Conte's mother had murmured. "I'd like to paint it—it looks like an old Spanish mission."

Today, for the first time, Conte had walked beyond the thick, old-fashioned stone walls. He had passed the old auditorium with its arched windows and tall bell tower, and then he had beheld a sickening sight.

Right in the center of what must once have been a rolling expanse of lawns, stood two new buildings, recent additions to the school. Conte had read about them in the newspaper. He blinked as he saw them. It was as if he were caught suddenly between two realities—a flaw in time.

The two new buildings were square, squat monsters with dark windows that reflected Conte's image a hundredfold. He shuddered. Some poor architect, he thought, must have labored for years to create such a total horror. Maybe it took a certain talent.

At last, as other students assembled, Conte moved inside one of the buildings. He felt as if unseen machines were sucking him in, just as invisible fans murmured and bubbled to keep the air cold and sterile.

Conte sat down in one of the upholstered seats, which faced a podium on the stage. He stretched out his legs, determined to appear casual and well adjusted. He knew a lot about body language. He glanced outside. Immediately his legs snapped back, his shoulders hunched together. Beyond those awful windows lay green sky, green pavement, green people. It was a sickening green world.

Out to the podium came a Mr. Rhinefinger, a small man who did what many small men do. He raised himself straight up on his toes. Small man, blessed with a huge voice, Rhinefinger proceeded to address the freshmen. Feedback echoed eerily through the PA system. Conte's ears rang. He felt as if he'd been stuffed inside a test tube and the cork tightly sealed.

Rhinefinger sustained an unsteady rhythm of voice and body, raising himself up as he stressed certain syllables. He seemed rather like a sailboat on a heavy sea.

"Welcome, young ladies and gentlemen to our beautiful *school*. *We*, the counseling staff, wish to *assure* you that here at Vista Mar the program is tailored to fit the needs of each *individual* student. We do not teach groups at Vista Mar. We teach *indivi-i-iduals*!"

The last word was drawn out for a full six seconds, keeping Rhinefinger on his toes so long it seemed he would soon flap his arms and fly off the stage.

Rhinefinger continued. He spoke of "our *beautiful* new buildings" obtained at "*enormous* cost" to the "good people of this *splendid* community." Then he spoke with great emotion of the good fortune of all who were gathered here to avail themselves of the "bounteous benefits of a free and democratic system of public education."

"Crap!" came a growl from beside Conte. He glanced at the owner of the voice, who thrust his head deep inside his coat collar, obviously wishing to remain incognito.

Rhinefinger now proceeded to intersperse his comments with gentle warnings and finally cold threats.

"We expect to be proud of our students," he said. "We prohibit smoking on school grounds. Anti-social behavior, criminal activities and *disrespect* will not be tolerated!"

At the word "disrespect," Rhinefinger again seemed ready for lift-off.

"Your grades," Rhinefinger said viciously, "will be given out each semester and recorded on a *computer*. Once recorded, there is no way on God's green earth that the grades can be changed. So don't beg and hound your teachers! Once the information is stored inside our *computer*, it's as invulnerable as . . . as . . ." He was stuck up there on his toes, without a word to get him down again. The person beside Conte began to giggle. The giggle ended in a snort.

"Next Monday," shouted out Rhinefinger, "when you come to school, go directly to your first class. Do not come to the office!" He gestured like a traffic cop. "Go directly to your first class."

Several hands shot up. Rhinefinger waved them aside and said, "Your programs have already been mailed to you."

Oh, yes, they have, thought Conte, shifting uncomfortably in his seat.

"Do not come to the counseling office on Monday!" Rhinefinger screamed, holding up both hands as if to ward off an impending flood. "The counseling staff will not have time to discuss your individual problems. Go to the classes as indicated on your program."

Yes, indeed, the programs had arrived in the mail. Two of them. One was addressed properly to Conte Mark. The other was sent to *Mark Conte*. Each program card listed a different schedule of classes and teachers.

Conte raised his hand again. Rhinefinger pretended not to notice. "Read your Freshman Orientation Booklets. Everything will be *crystal* clear," he said.

Now Rhinefinger boomed out with evident pleasure. "To demonstrate our interest in each *individual* student," he said grandly, "I shall call each of you to the podium, where you may pick up your Freshman Orientation Booklet and *shake my hand*."

A unanimous groan rumbled through the auditorium, beginning at the back and cresting like an ocean wave near the stage. Above the uproar Rhinefinger called out, "Those of you whose last names begin with *A* through *L* will be assigned to me for counseling. During the year I will see each and every one of you. Those whose last names begin with *M* through *Z* will be assigned to Miss Worfenstein."

The owner of that name bobbed up, smiled, and Conte had the vague impression of a beaming sun face, like the ones on posters advertising flights to Mexico.

"Our Miss Worfenstein," said Rhinefinger, "is always available."

A lecherous laugh issued from somewhere along the side of the auditorium. Hastily Rhinefinger began calling the roll.

The boy beside Conte sighed deeply and grumbled, "What makes him think we want to shake his hand?"

Conte shrugged. Then he said, "I'll bet you five bucks he gets my last name mixed up with my first."

The boy's eyes, like narrow slits, peered out from under a long shock of molasses brown hair. "You're on."

"Where's your cash?" asked Conte.

"Ha! I got plenty. Where's yours?"

"In my pocket."

"Show it." The boy's eyes flickered. They were the color of amber.

Conte showed him the five dollar bill, hard earned by helping his dad. "This five bucks," he said, "represents about twenty-five fence post holes. Work. New house. Moving in—it's for the birds."

"Yeah," came from beneath the shag of hair. "What's your name, anyway? Rumplestiltskin?" The boy's shoulders shook with repressed laughter.

"Conte."

"You're putting me on."

"No. See? Here's my ID. Conte Mark. But Rhine-finger will call me 'Mark Conte.' You'll see. It happens a lot."

"But your name's on the computer," objected shaggy-head. "They even get my name right. It's Kurt Zelinko-witz. Computers don't make mistakes."

"Oh, don't they?" Conte said sharply. Zelinkowitz just sat there, withdrawn.

Conte looked at him more closely. Hair sprouted from a large hole in his jeans, right at the thigh. His jacket of brown leather was torn and stained. One of his tennis shoes was lacking the whole toepiece. He was obviously a rich kid.

"Only rich kids can get away with looking like bums," Conte's mother once said. "Get a regular kid or a really poor one looking like that, and all the old biddies cluck their tongues."

She never identified the "old biddies." It was just her phrase for anybody she was mad at. When his dad got laid off from work, she had gotten very red in the face and said, "Old biddies!" Then she had started to cry.

Conte leaned forward, listening for his name. He could already feel that five bucks in his hand, and he knew exactly how he'd spend it. It was a sure thing. Yup. Loudly Mr. Rhinefinger called out, "*Mark Conte!*"

With a grin at Kurt Zelinkowitz, Conte ambled up the aisle to get his booklet and handshake. Rhinefinger's hand was moist and flabby. Conte opened his mouth to explain that his name had been reversed, and that furthermore, he had received an extra program card in the mail. But as their hands met, Rhinefinger had already seized another booklet and was calling out another name. To top it off, he gave Conte a shove and muttered, "Get going, kid!"

Down the aisle again, Conte's fingers itched to collect his five bucks. With it, at last, he'd get that Comminger Catalogue Company off his back. But Zelinkowitz, the rat, was gone.

Now, it might seem that the disappearance of Zelinkowitz was a slight and trivial matter. Not so. Zelinkowitz's treachery was the last straw. Enough now. Too much. The droning air conditioner, the sickening green windows seemed to move in on Conte.

As he walked toward home, his anger mounted. Stop! Conte inwardly commanded the world. Get offa my back! Stop!

Like a red button pushed in his brain, something was released. A small spark ignited. It began immediately to feed itself on Conte's anger.

Those hideous buildings and that suffocating green room!

The hypocrisy of Rhinefinger!

Kirkland Company!

Zelinkowitz, the rat!

And most of all, the Comminger Catalogue Company, which was still hounding him, attacking him with a stream of literature that came addressed to him as "Dear Acct. No. a6401btx." Almost daily it assaulted him with enticing values, and notices that urged him to pay, warned him to pay, and threatened him with legal action. They charged him two and three times for the same item, charged him interest, reversed his payment figures. It was all done by computer, of course.

If a man's home is his castle, then a boy's school ought to be his refuge from the hostile, impersonal world of machines. In school one should find personal interest and concern. Right?

Conte, puffing from his uphill climb, could clearly envision how his life was being arranged by that clacking computer stationed somewhere at Vista Mar High.

It would punch and plan, shuffle and rattle and finally *spit him out*, for he was only a card. Only a card. If ever his card got lost, he might as well be dead. It wasn't enough that you were breathing and taking up space. If nobody had a card on file for you, you didn't exist.

But . . . but . . . if somebody had two cards for you . . . why then . . . then there were two of you, right?

Oh, oh, Rhinefinger, oh, Vista Mar High and all computers everywhere, just wait!

He, Conte Mark, was going to wipe out that computer at Vista Mar High. Oh, the delicious irony of it. The computer had sown the seeds of its own destruction. By printing out two program cards, it had played right into Conte's hands. Whoever said computers don't make mistakes?

With just a little maneuvering, he'd get himself graduated from that high school not in the four years it usually took but in two years flat. Basically, all he had to do was to continue to be counted as two different people, taking two different sets of classes. At the appropriate time it ought to be simple to have the credits on the two cards added together. The reversed name would simply be corrected. The units would be added together. Then the computer would print out a STUDIES COMPLETED card and type his name on a master list of GRADUATES. And Conte would be on his way to bigger and better things.

Afterward, when his files were stamped and his diploma in his hand, Conte would march into that office and watch their mouths fall open when they realized that their disgusting machine had made a spectacular boo-boo. He knew from his dad that people would do nearly anything rather than admit a mistake. It would be too late to change anything.

2 Greg, the Perfect Ally

From his mom there was a note on the kitchen table. "GONE JUNK COLLECTING."

Conte got a quart of milk from the refrigerator. He drank long, luxurious gulps straight from the carton, savoring the beauty of this moment, embellishing his plan. When it was all done, perhaps he'd leave a printed message somewhere, as burglars with a creative flourish sometimes leave clever notes. His would say, THE MARK OF CONTE!

He wondered what Mom would say if he told her. Would she get that gleam in her eyes and giggle like a girl, declaring, "Serves them right, the old biddies!"

Or, more likely, she'd give him that hard look and yell, "Conte Mark, you will do no such thing, do you hear me? No such thing!" She'd stand there glaring at him. She'd make outrageous threats.

That was the thing about his mom. She was inconsistent. She'd get uptight about the craziest things, like people drinking out of milk cartons. Other times she'd pull pranks of her own. Once she had dyed their whole dinner purple, everything from soup to cake. You could never tell how she'd react. She herself admitted, with a trace of pride, "Of course I'm inconsistent. What's the fun in being predictable?"

Well, she was an artist and a little—well, different. Conte decided not to tell her. Later, presented with the *fait accompli*, his parents would do nothing. After all, he'd have found a creative solution to his own problem. That's what they were always telling him to do. For now, his plan would remain a secret.

But as Conte sat in his room pondering his plan, it became clear that he would need help. On his desk lay the two computer-printed program cards. There were countless details to consider. The main problem, of course, lay in the obvious fact that he couldn't be in two places at once, and that he must keep his two identities separate.

Conte sighed and went out into the backyard, where Dag, his Great Dane, was an uneasy captive. Dag systematically patrolled the four corners of the yard, then ran up the wooden deck off the family room where he delivered a howling reproach. He was a restless dog, with many unfulfilled psychological needs. Whatever Dag wanted out of life, he certainly wasn't getting it.

The moment Conte came out, Dag galloped over and pinned his master to the wall. The dog painted Conte's cheeks with dozens of furious, slippery kisses. Conte tried gently to fend him off. At last he was forced to resort to insults. He gave the dog a push and said scornfully, "Get offa me, you pervert."

Dag retreated, head down, tail dragging. Several minutes later, dog and master were reconciled. Dag retrieved the old slobbery tennis ball for Conte. They developed a quiet, easy rhythm. While he threw the ball again and again, Conte pondered his options.

He could use a disguise for one of his selves. Conte Mark would be the quiet intellectual, who wore dress shirts and maybe even a tie. *Mark Conte* would be suave and witty, casual and red hot on the saxophone.

This double identity thing had possibilities, all right. No—no—it was better with no disguise at all. At a school the size of Vista Mar a person could get lost. The kids wouldn't care or even notice. Half the time the guys called each other by their last names anyhow. Nobody would bother to ask which was which. That was precisely what he was trying to prove. When students are treated like numbers and teachers act like robots, who needs a disguise? But how in the world would he handle two whole programs at once?

Again Conte threw the ball. It sailed clear over the fence into the next yard. In that moment Conte knew he had found his ally. Greg Gaff.

Conte sighed. Greg was the perfect ally. He was also the most boring person on earth. In fact, Greg's whole family moved so slowly they seemed to be living in a different dimension.

But Greg was a junior. He knew the ropes. He had an old car and a driver's license. Most important of all, Conte had the feeling he could trust Greg Gaff. Greg gave off vibrations that said plainly, "I may be a jerk, but I'm loyal and trustworthy."

Conte got his Freshman Orientation Booklet and went next door. He knocked. At last Greg emerged, yawning and shaking his head as if he had sand in his ears.

One thing you had to say for Greg Gaff. He was a good listener. He didn't interrupt. In fact, as Conte neared the end of his explanation, it seemed Greg had fallen asleep.

"Hey, you OK?"

But Greg did not answer. His face became flushed. Like a fish out of water, he seemed to have trouble breathing.

"You OK?" Conte repeated with a feeling of alarm. Maybe the kid was really sick.

Greg nodded to himself, as old men nod over their memories. Suddenly he gave a yelp, slapped his thigh, and burst out laughing.

"You—you like the idea?" Conte asked weakly.

"By George!" Greg screamed out. "All my life I have waited—for—the perfect—perfect plot."

"Plot?"

"Plot! Plan! *Prank*," Greg shouted, and now he began to pace. "Way-to-show-them. Beat-the-hell-out-of-the-system. The-perfect-rip-off. All my life I've waited and," he stopped and faced Conte squarely, "you've got it," he said.

A fantastic change had come over Greg. Suddenly he was animated, limber, exuberant. His eyes glowed, his voice rang as he repeated again and again, "By George, you've got it."

Conte asked, "Does that mean you'll help me?"

"I will."

"Do you think it'll work?"

"Of course!"

"Really?"

Greg frowned. "I don't know. Maybe. It could be dangerous," he added.

"How so?"

"You'll have to tamper with the computer at least once. I think that's called vandalism. I won't get involved in anything like that," Greg said firmly. "I've got too much to lose. If I got in trouble with the fuzz, my folks would take away my car, my pad, my equipment—everything. Whatever happens," he said, "you'll have to take full responsibility."

Conte was astonished. This kid was beginning to sound like a member of the Junior Mafia.

"All right," he said. "I'll keep your name out of it."

"Would you sign a document to that effect?"

"For Pete's sake, Greg!" Conte shouted. "Do we have to get a stupid lawyer?"

"I guess we could just shake on it," Greg conceded, and they did. "Now," Greg said, "come on down to my room. *Partner*."

Downstairs they went, where Greg had himself a sweet setup. He had a regular apartment down there, with two beds and a sofa, a separate workroom complete with printing press and photo equipment and a darkroom made out of a spare closet.

Greg tipped over a chair to let the debris slide to the floor, then he shoved a mass of clothes and books down under the bed. It warmed Conte's heart to see the mess. Maybe Greg was normal after all.

"Now," Greg said briskly, "let's see your program, your schedule of classes, your computer slips."

Greg had this maddening way of repeating himself. Conte wondered what caused it, but decided to ignore it. Having a psychologist for a father was sometimes a nuisance. It alerted him to people's peculiarities and often tempted him to try to solve their problems. Well, not this time, Conte thought grimly.

He took the schedules from his pocket and laid them out on Greg's desk. For several minutes both of them studied the lists.

	Mark, Conte ⌗3762			Conte, Mark ⌗3449	
1.	Swm	Brwn	1.	Swm	Brwn
2.	Hst	Soms	2.	Alg	Merm
3.	Eng	Bkfd	3.	Bio	Dean
4.	Bnd	Mott	4.	Bnd	Mott
5.	Alg	Merm	5.	Hst	Mors
6.	Bio	Ptsn	6.	Eng	Ahrn

Greg translated the computer-coded words into plain English and rewrote the schedules onto a large piece of paper:

	Mark, Conte ⌗3762			Conte, Mark ⌗3449	
1.	Swimming	Coach Brown	1.	Swimming	Coach Brown
2.	History	Miss Sommers	2.	Algebra	Miss Merriman
3.	English	Mrs. Bickford	3.	Biology	Mr. Dean
4.	Band	Mr. Mott	4.	Band	Mr. Mott
5.	Algebra	Miss Merriman	5.	History	Mr. Morse
6.	Biology	Mr. Peterson	6.	English	Mrs. Aherne

"Your problem," said Greg, vigorously shaking his head, "is obvious. Conte Mark cannot have the same teachers as *Mark Conte*."

"So, *Mark Conte* can't take band." Conte flipped through the Orientation Booklet. "It says here there's a class called special project art. It's taught fourth period. Listen to this! 'A course designed for the experienced art student who wishes to pursue an independent art project. Class meetings are informal.'"

"That means you don't have to go to class," Greg said. "It's perfect."

"The only thing," Conte said gloomily, "is that I'm not experienced. I've never taken art. I'll have to fake it."

"Listen, artists are always faking it. That's nothing new. They're all a bunch of . . ."

"My mother," Conte said coldly, "happens to be an artist."

Abruptly Greg changed the subject.

"Your biggest problem," said Greg, "is that both of your programs have Coach Brown for swimming. That will present a difficulty, a hazard . . ."

"Can't one of me just change to another period for swimming?" Conte asked.

"Not at all," said Greg, hitching up his trouser legs like a man of sixty. Now that Conte thought of it, most of Greg's mannerisms were like those of an old man. He hardly seemed like a kid at all, but like one of those storybook characters sprouted full grown and wrinkled out of a walnut.

"Coach Brown," continued Greg, "is a strange character. You know how some people never forget a face? Well, Coach Brown never forgets a stroke. He prides himself on that. So you can't deceive him, con him, get around him. . . ."

"Well then, I just won't take swimming," Conte said.

"You've got to. Every freshman has to take swimming."

"How come?"

Greg began to pace the floor. "Why do you think? *Not* for the sake of the students, that's for sure. It's because the school has a deal with the Ace Laundry to deliver 600 fresh towels every morning. That's why you have to swim. To keep the Ace Laundry in business."

"That's ridiculous," snapped Conte.

"Oh, is it? Is it? Who do you think owns the Ace Laundry? A. Dunlop Peeches, that's who. A. Dunlop Peeches, who also happens to be a member of the Vista Mar School Board. Get it?"

"I get it," Conte said glumly. Things were even worse than he'd thought.

"The whole system," said Greg, "stinks of corruption. But we're gonna show them. Let's get on with it. Now, if you were handicapped. . . ."

"That's hard to fake," objected Conte.

"Maybe we could get help from Charlotta Jones." Greg's eyes were suddenly mellow and dreamy.

"Who's Charlotta Jones?"

"But we'd better save her for a real emergency."

"Who's Charlotta?"

"Charlotta," said Greg with a sigh, "is a nice girl, but . . ." He shook his head. "Never mind. You'll know soon enough. She's always in the band room. Now, as for algebra . . ."

"One of me will have to take a different teacher."

"No way."

"What?"

"Miss Merriman is the only algebra teacher. She's got a monopoly on freshman algebra. I think it's all she knows."

"Then how in the world can I go through with this?"

Suddenly the whole plan seemed absurd and impossible. Conte felt again that the world was crowding in on him. His face was hot. His palms itched, a sure sign of impending panic. It would never work. It was just one of those wild, wonderful ideas people get, but when it comes to really doing it. . . .

"It won't work," Conte said heatedly. "I mean, this Miss Merriman would have to be blind and semi-conscious . . ."

"You've just about got it."

"Oh, Greg, this is a rotten idea. I mean, how can I keep it up for two years? I've got to take swimming, you said, but there's only one coach. I've got to have algebra or I'll never get into higher math, and there's only one teacher. How can it possibly work?"

"Because of the system, Conte! It will work because nobody really cares about the individual student. Everybody tries to set things up for his own personal, selfish reasons. That's why you can get away with it."

"But all the arrangements—we don't have much time."

Greg nodded vigorously. "You can make changes in your program up until the third week of school. All you have to do is get in good with some of the teachers, and they'll excuse you from class for all sorts of things. We'll find some more 'special project classes' for you to take. Listen, one kid I heard about got physiology credit for just keeping track of his diet, his cavities, and the rate of growth of his toenails. No kidding. They'll give you credit for all sorts of odd things."

Conte narrowed his eyes and began pacing, hands in his pockets, like a spy. "Maybe I'll have to get a disguise for one of me. You know—different clothes. Think I could grow long sideburns? I can't go around wearing a mask . . ."

For several moments Greg rocked back and forth, pondering. Then softly, reverently, he said, "That's it. Of course. For P.E. let *Mark Conte* stay in swimming. Conte Mark will take fencing."

"Fencing!" Conte leaped to his feet. "I don't want to get cut up!"

"Don't be stupid," Greg snapped. "Sure, that's it."

"But how can I take fencing and swimming at the same time?"

"You won't," Greg said flatly. "There's a special class called 'Early Bird P.E.' You'll take that."

"But you said *every* freshman has to swim," Conte argued.

"*Except* for those who take Early Bird P.E.," Greg said. "They're pushing the Early Bird classes. One of the coaches got a government grant—lots of money— experimental program."

Conte flipped through the booklet. "They don't teach fencing for Early Bird P.E.," he said. "They just teach fencing sixth period, and it's not for freshmen."

"I know that," Greg said. "We're just going to have to see to it that certain changes are made in the curriculum."

Conte felt himself wavering between panic and joy. Either Greg Gaff was a real psycho with delusions of grandeur—or he was a real cool cat and an organizational genius.

"We'll try it your way," Conte said solemnly. "How do we begin?"

3 The Curriculum-Changing Caper

The plan was still incomplete, but as Conte sauntered home he felt confident. They were on the right track. Together he and Greg would cut through red tape and get down to basics. What was basic about school? Roll call.

The first thing every kindergartener learns is to RE-PORT FOR ROLL CALL. It is drummed into his little head. Even if he has to leave ten minutes later, first comes roll call.

Why? So his name gets onto the Daily Attendance Sheet.

Why's that important?

So the school gets its money from the state.

Who needs it? The teachers and principals, so the school can survive, so the PTA can keep on meeting and selling donuts, so the custodians can continue to play poker in the mop closet and dads can look forward to homecoming games each fall.

That, in a nutshell, is why people have to report for roll call, and why Conte would have to say "Here!" in twelve different classes each day. It would take a bit of organizing. In some classes, like study hall, you could just sign in and then leave. In his other classes, Conte would alternate between actually being present and offering some appropriate excuse. The list of possible excuses was intriguing—dentist appointments, skinned knees, snake bite, broken collarbone, lost book, injured bird who needed medical aid, participation in a balloon launch, a paper drive, a TP'ing of the rival school . . . he'd think of something.

The algebra class would be tough, but according to Greg, Miss Merriman was hard of hearing, weak in the eyes, and slow on the draw. By the time she realized the same kid was in two of her classes, they'd have thought of something else; Greg *guaranteed* it.

Now, while Greg worked on his plan to introduce Early Bird fencing into the curriculum, Conte went to work on his mom to solve at least one of his class problems.

He found her home and in the kitchen, barefoot and wearing her old Levis. That was a good sign. It sometimes seemed to Conte that he had two mothers in one form. The first wore jeans and fooled with kooky projects that involved all kinds of metal junk. Her junk sculptures jiggled and rattled. She said they made STATE-MENTS. Sometimes she had Conte install winking little lights for her.

The other mom wore pantsuits or even dresses. She polished her nails and pinned up her hair. She rushed off to meetings and parties and said things like, "You'd better take a shower, young man," or "I expect to see your room cleaned by dinnertime." Fortunately, this mom didn't appear as often as the other one.

"How'd it go?" Mom asked, meaning the orientation, meaning further, are you going to continue to be miserable and moody? Or are you going to snap out of it now that school's started?

"I think I'll like school," Conte said.

"Hey—great! Did you make new friends?"

"Not exactly." Conte glowered at the thought of Zelinkowitz. He'd tend to that rat later. Casually he continued, "I was over at Greg's this afternoon. He's not so bad."

"Well, that's great, I thought you told me last week he was strange—like a fish, didn't you say?"

"Yeah, well, I guess that's because his mom's an ich-thyologist or a marine biologist, or whatever you call it. They got a lot of fish tanks around the house, and I guess when you've had to live with fish all your life like that, it does something to you."

"I know what you mean," his mother said, nodding.

"Mrs. Gaff seems very nice but she's—well, she gasps a lot, and she talks so *slowly*."

"Greg told me how I can get an extra class into my schedule. I have to take Early Bird P.E. Greg's going to take it, too. He drives to school. So that's no problem. I could go with him."

"Wait a minute! What time is this 'early bird' thing?"

"Seven in the morning," Conte said quickly, "but I'd get my own breakfast, and the special class I want to take is called multi-media art."

His mother did not look at him, but she stopped moving for a long moment. "Well," she said briskly, "it's all right with me, Conte. I really don't mind if you want to have to get up that early."

She sniffed slightly and went back to her cooking and chopping. Several minutes later she said, "Multi-media, you say? Sounds interesting. Any idea what sort of project you'd do?"

"Well, I'm not sure yet. I've been making a few sketches . . ." Liar! screamed a small voice. Well, so he'd make some sketches tonight—big deal. "I guess I'll use different media. Thought I'd try metal and string. Will you start saving old orange juice cans for me? Of course, I'll need a note from you with permission to take Early Bird P.E."

"OK," said Mom. "I'll write you a note."

Who'd make the switch—Conte Mark or *Mark*

Conte? He'd decide later, maybe ask Mom to sign her name *Mrs. Conte.* Yeah, she'd go for that sort of prank. People were always getting his name mixed up, and more than once the secretary in the attendance office at school had phoned and asked for "Mrs. Conte."

Flexibility that was called, and that was the keynote of his father's life. So flexible was he that he refused to eat the same thing for breakfast twice in a row. He didn't want to cultivate a habit, he said. So flexible was he that when Kirkland Corporation decided it no longer needed a psychologist to test prospective employees— a computer could do it better—he had hardly minded.

"Let us still remain flexible," he had said. "I will adopt a new line of work. There's a fellow in California that I interviewed for K.C. a couple of years ago. K.C. rejected him. The test showed that he was brilliant, creative, and friendly. They were looking for someone different. Well, this fellow, Anthony Fisher, went on to California to become the head sales manager of a huge company. After that he decided to form his own company. He finds executive jobs for people. He wrote to me. Said he was so grateful to me because K.C. rejected him, that if I ever wanted to change my line of work I should look him up. I called him today. He as much as offered me a partnership. We're going to California!"

It had been easy for Conte's dad, therefore, to make

the sudden change. Mom hadn't seemed to mind either. She just packed up her junk and found a house with a nice screened sun porch where she could "create." The only one who had been upset about the move was Conte.

It wasn't that he was really so crazy about Texas. They'd only lived there for three years, having moved before that from Oregon, and before that from San Francisco. But—well, things were just starting to take hold for him in Texas. He'd been student director of the school band. He'd expected that honor to follow him to the high school. And he had friends. Not many, to be sure, and sometimes they were kind of kinky, but they were his friends, and he knew what to expect of them. Then there was Karen, cool and distant until she found out he was moving and then—oh, man—she changed.

So, summer had been a drag. He helped his folks fix up the yard. He saw Greg a couple of times. Mostly he hung around fixing his stereo, making himself a control panel and fooling around with the telephones, which made his Mom awful mad. (He liked to rewire things, especially telephones.)

He missed his friends, Cornball Charlie, Hairy Bob, Stanley the Bass. They all had nicknames like that. They called him The Mark. Well, it was all gone, gone, and he had been depressed.

"When school starts," his dad had said reassuringly,

"you'll feel better. You'll adjust. It takes time."

"I'm fine!" Conte insisted. "I like it here!"

"Sure."

The trouble with having a psychologist for a father was that he could see right through you. "Hang loose," his dad advised. "Stay flexible."

On Wednesday, only two days after The Birth of the Great Idea, all systems were "go." When school started on the following Monday, a new course would be part of the curriculum. Conte had always wondered how curriculum decisions were made. Now he knew. And his respect for Greg Gaff had increased one hundred percent.

"It's all set, in the bag," Greg said excitedly. "All we have to do is to get thirty kids signed up to take Early Bird fencing."

"But how did you do it?"

"Just used my head, my bean, my imagination." Greg lay back on his elbows on the lawn in Conte's yard. As a symbol of friendship, Dag slammed into Greg, knocked him flat, then proceeded to bathe him in kisses.

"Get that beast away from me!" screamed Greg. He brushed himself off, then began to explain, frowning and rubbing his chin.

"See, Mr. Gireaux teaches French, mainly, but he's a nut about fencing. So he teaches one fencing class almost every semester. They had him scheduled to teach fencing sixth period, with third period free. I knew he'd hate that."

"But why?"

"He likes to leave school early, because of the traffic."

"What traffic?"

"Other bikes." Greg shook his head. "Gireaux rides a motorbike. Likes to get out of the parking lot before the traffic. So I knew he'd like to change sixth period fencing to Early Bird, then teach another French class during third period. That way he could go home right after lunch."

"And he went for it?"

"Did he ever! Especially when I suggested it could be co-ed."

"Who ever heard of co-ed P.E.?"

"That's the beauty of it. It's a completely new idea. Just what he needs. He's taking some kind of an education class at night. Has to write a term paper. You know, that psychological garbage. Now he can do his paper on 'The Social and Psychological Effects of Co-Educational Fencing.' He's really turned on about it."

"Sounds terrific," Conte said. "But how are we going to get thirty people to take fencing at seven in the morning?"

"Simple," Greg said. "There's already two of us. Now all we have to do is get one guy signed up. The rest will follow."

"Who's the guy—Robert Redford?"

"Just about. His name's Rob Owens. The chicks are crazy about him. I figure all we have to do is . . ."

"Just spread the word!" Conte shouted. "Hey, you *are* brilliant. When do we start?"

"Today. We'll go down to the school and sign up for fencing."

"Wait a minute. How do we make this guy Owens take the Early Bird fencing class?"

"Good question. We'll think about it on the way to the school. I've got to get my program change approved by my counselor. You might as well wait until we get some more details worked out before you make any changes. You can do it all at once.

They climbed into Greg's car. The car itself seemed to know every inch of the way, so deftly did it round the turns until it came screeching into the parking lot.

"Hey!" shouted Conte. "I've got it! We just tell this guy Rob Owens that twenty chicks are taking this fencing class. Does he go for women?"

"Does he ever!"

"So, we just tell him . . ."

"No," Greg said.

"No?" echoed Conte.

"You don't tell Rob Owens anything. You have to get to Downer."

"Who the heck is Downer?" yelled Conte. "Why's

everything so complicated around here?"

"Listen," said Greg slowly, "there are certain *procedures*. Every society, every town, every school has certain customs and procedures. At Vista Mar, if you want to get something from Rob Owens—if you even just want to talk to Rob Owens—you go see Dennis Downer. That's the way it's done."

Conte clenched his teeth. Why was every little thing so complicated? It would take him years to feel familiar here. These kids were really creeps.

"What are you going to do while I'm seeing my counselor?" Greg asked.

"I'll wait for you in the library."

"What'll you do there? Won't you be bored? Will you read?"

"I'll write dirty words on the wall!" Conte snapped. Immediately he was sorry for being so nasty. He thrust his hands into his pockets and gave an arrogant swing to his walk. Greg was the only person in this whole crummy town who'd even talk to him. Now Greg was probably mad at him.

It was just as well, Conte grumbled to himself, that he'd be getting out of high school early. All his life, it seemed, he'd been looking for friends. Real friends, not just guys to hang around with, but good friends who cared about the same things he did. He remembered way back in kindergarten, how the teacher had given him a queer look and told his mother, "You must understand, Mrs. Mark, that most little boys don't happen to share Conte's interests."

His first grade teacher had made the same sort of little "ahem" noises before she told his mother, "On an emotional level Conte responds better to adults than to children his own age."

"You mean," his Mom had said icily, "that the other little boys want to roar around and punch each other all the time, while Conte would rather learn and converse and do interesting things?"

"Well, *ahem*, yes," said the teacher. "I suppose that's it."

His parents had worried about him. Conte knew it. Then, whenever the opportunity arose, they told him reassuring things. They were proud of him, they said. They enjoyed being with him. As he grew older, he'd find other kids he'd like being with, kids who would share his interests. By the time he got to high school, they said, he'd have no more conflicts.

Ha! Sullenly Conte ambled up to the desk. He asked to see the catalogues of various colleges and whatever career planning information was available. He kept his face down, lips set into a sneer, eyes assuming a sideways, slitted glance. He felt like one of those haughty male lions one sees in the zoo.

"I won't show you where anything is," said a distinct

and angry feminine voice, "unless you ask nicely."

"What? What the h . . ."

No girl could get away with talking like that, like something out of a hundred-year-old novel—but . . . but he took one look at her and figured she could get away with anything she pleased. Anything.

"Where are the catalogues, please?" he said softly, grinning foolishly. Inside he felt like—oh, oh, his insides were as tangled as a mass of Chinese noodles. No longer the lion, he felt like a fawn. Yes, a fawn.

"Here you are," she said, pointing to an alcove with table and chairs and shelves neatly stacked with catalogues.

And Conte sat down, watching the girl as she walked away. Dreamily he began to browse through the catalogues one after the other, keeping the girl always in the corner of his gaze. Suddenly the world was moving far more slowly than before. All sorts of sounds—insects, birds, little chirping voices—were floating around outside. So struck was Conte with the wonder of it that he nearly missed the item in the catalogue. But three letters stood out prominently enough in his memory to make him do a double take. Those three letters were HIC. Those three letters meant all the difference between a plan doomed to failure and one that was sure to succeed.

4 Introducing the HIC

HIC, as Conte had known for years, stood for High Intelligence Child. Conte remembered that afternoon long ago when they were still living in San Francisco. He was in first grade. A messenger summoned him to the office.

Conte went cheerfully, thinking he knew what the summons was all about. Just a week earlier he had done something a little unusual even for him. In the school library he had seen a wooden box with a sign that said: "Suggested Titles." He sometimes saw teachers filling out order slips for books. So Conte had decided to help himself. He wrote out an order for a set of the *Worldwide Encyclopedia* for his classroom. He also ordered a copy of *The Challenge of Hydro-Electric Energy*. That one was for the school library.

As it turned out, the summons was not about his book order. But, as he learned later, it was prompted by his order.

The secretary, Miss Brown, greeted him in her baby-talk, cuddly-wuddly way. "Oh, it's Conte Mark! How is he today? Is he fine? Oh, lovely. Did he come to see our friend Mr. Anderson?"

Everybody knew that Mr. Anderson was nobody's friend. Conte told the secretary, "I've come to see the school psychologist."

Miss Brown's smile froze solidly on her lips. "Come in, Conte. Mr. Anderson, this is Conte Mark. You and he are going to play some games together. Won't that be fun?"

Mr. Anderson held out his hand. He told Conte to sit down and make himself comfortable. He told Conte not to be frightened. Conte only smiled.

For half an hour or so Conte proceeded to put pegs into holes. He made designs out of colored blocks. He answered questions about pictures and ink blots. In fact, he played just about the same kind of games he'd been playing with his dad for years.

Then came the serious questions.

"Now, Conte, tell me, what makes a car go?"

"Do you mean how do you *start* a car?" Conte asked. "You start it with a key, and it's run by gasoline. The key activates the spark plug, which spark is caught by the generator, which turns the belt . . ." He paused. "Or did you mean how to *build* a car?"

A week later his parents received a letter from the

school, informing them that Conte had been designated as a HIC.

Being a HIC had never meant much to Conte. But now, in the booklet titled "State Graduation Requirements," Conte had seen the following printed announcement:

A high school student who has been identified as a HIC may, with the approval of his counselor, complete certain courses by working independently under the supervision of a faculty member. Students will receive full credit for satisfactory completion of projects thus undertaken and approved by the faculty supervisor. A student may take no more than two (2) HIC courses during any one semester.

Conte fully understood the significance of this information. All he had to do was adjust his programs so that he could alternate between regular courses and HIC courses.

Unwittingly he gasped and spoke aloud, "I'm a HIC!"

"How do you do," said the girl, having come to shelve some books. "I'm Pamela Patterson."

"Conte Mark," he introduced himself.

"Patterson, Pamela," she said with a grin. "Do you always talk backwards?"

"No, I do," he countered, grinning back at her, proceeding to walk backwards as he spoke, until he bumped into a fierce-looking librarian who gave him a good piece of her mind without even uttering a word. Her look said it all—he was an idiot.

At that moment Greg arrived, gave Conte the "victory" sign, and together they dropped the first bombshell. "Guess who," Greg said to Pamela, "is taking what class for Early Bird P.E.? Mixed P.E.? Would you believe—fencing?"

Conte added, "Would you believe—Rob Owens?"

The effect was instantaneous. Pamela Patterson's face went pale, then pink. She rushed off, and from behind the stacks Greg and Conte heard a flustery whispering, giggling, shuffling, until the fierce librarian clapped her hands together smartly and firmly. But the die was cast. The seeds were sown.

On Thursday morning about fifty girls (all chasing Rob Owens) and about twenty boys (chasing the fifty girls) created a minor riot. They stormed the attendance office to get their programs changed. All signed up for Early Bird fencing.

School officials were astounded. What could it mean? The vice-principal immediately prepared a report for the school board. The school board requested additional funds from Washington. One member urged that the district consider letting all students start their day at seven, since this particular generation of students was apparently starved for learning.

A young English teacher got wind of the mass move toward fencing. Convinced that it was the beginning of a new fad, she wrote an article called, "Revival of the Ancient Combative Arts," and sent it to *Campus* magazine.

Mr. Gireaux figured he was now the most popular teacher on campus. He bought a wild new jacket, a purple helmet, and started making passes at the history teacher, Miss Sommers.

Within a few months, the Early Bird fencing class at Vista Mar High was to become a model for other programs. It was written up in educational journals. Student teachers were sent to observe. Only Conte and Greg knew that the entire fencing movement had been possible only because Coach Gireaux happened to own a motorcycle.

On Thursday afternoon Greg and Conte solidified their plans and went over what had been done. Greg sat with his arms folded across his chest. "I talked to Downer. You must understand that he and Owens have the perfect symbiotic relationship."

Conte nodded. "I see. They support each other."

"Exactly. They're always together. See, the chicks are crazy about Owens."

"But why? What's he got?"

"Good looks," said Greg. "And money. He's played some bit parts in movies and done some TV commercials."

"Why does he need Downer?"

"Oh, because Downer has a friend called Flint, and Flint has got the brains. If you wanna know who really runs this school, there's a trio: Flint, Downer, and Zelinkowitz . . ."

"I know that rat Zelinkowitz!" Conte cried. "He owes me five bucks."

Greg smiled gently, wisely. "You, too? Listen, the best advice I can give you about Flint, Downer, and Zelinkowitz is to stay away from them. I'm not even sure what they'll be doing this semester. Last year they took over the john by the west corner of the gym."

"What are you talking about?" Conte cried. He wondered how a newcomer could survive in this crazy town.

"They'd stand by the door to the bathroom and collect a quarter from anybody who wanted to go in. Don't you see? It was mostly for the smokers."

"Pot smokers?"

"Yeah. And just regular cigarettes, too, I guess."

"Hey, Greg, have you ever tried pot?"

Greg's face got that puffed, red look again. He wagged his head in the now familiar sand-in-ears manner, but he didn't answer. Conte shrugged. He and the gang back home used to talk about things like that all the time. Well, it just showed that he and Greg were only business associates, nothing more.

"Anyhow," Greg continued, "Downer and Owens are going to take Early Bird fencing to get in with all those girls, so we've got ourselves a class. Now, let's work up the rest of your schedule."

"It's beautiful," Conte said proudly. After his first awareness of the HIC program and what it could mean, he had told Greg about it only briefly. Now he had worked out most of the details. He took up the large poster board, which had been purchased for this purpose, and proceeded to write out his newly conceived program:

Mark, Conte ⌗3762	Conte, Mark ⌗3449
Counselor—Worfenstein Early Bird P.E.	Counselor—Rhinefinger
1. Study Hall Adams	1. Swimming Coach Brown
2. History Sommers	2. Algebra (HIC)
3. English (HIC)	3. Biology Dean
4. Band Mott	4. Art—Special Mr. Stanley
5. Algebra Merriman	5. History (HIC)
6. Biology (HIC)	6. English Aherne

Conte stood back, filled with admiration for his handiwork. Impatiently Greg tapped his foot. "Why did you underline some of the classes?"

"Those underlined," Conte replied, "are the classes I have to attend every day." He picked up a broken yardstick, and using it for a pointer, explained.

"My day begins at seven. By the courtesy of one Greg Gaff, I get to school for Early Bird fencing. First period, I sign in for study hall, run back to the gym for swimming, and," he added, beaming, "I do the whole thing with fourteen minutes to spare."

"Incredible." Greg nodded sleepily.

"It's all a question of control." Conte tapped the pointer. "Details are important. Like, every morning I wear my swim trunks under my school clothes. For fencing, I put on the uniform *over* my school clothes. We get ten minutes to change before and after class—right?"

"Right. Correct. Exactly."

"I'll allow the ten minutes before fencing for unforseen problems. But after fencing, I just pull off my uniform and stuff it into my locker. That takes thirty-five seconds. Allowing for a certain amount of traffic, it'll take exactly two minutes and fifteen seconds to get to study hall."

"Did you time it?"

"Yesterday, with a stopwatch. It takes ten seconds to sign my name. Two minutes and fifteen seconds to run back to the gym. In fifty seconds I pull off my clothes and run to the pool. Only six minutes have passed since the end of fencing class. The first bell hasn't even rung yet. It won't ring for four more minutes. That, plus the ten minutes dressing time allowed for swimming, gives me fourteen minutes to spare."

Conte was breathless, as if he had just done it. But determinedly, he continued. "For second period, I go to history with Miss Sommers. *Mark Conte* takes algebra as a HIC course. For HIC courses you read on your own and do special, advanced projects, and report to your faculty supervisor once a week. I can do that between classes, or during one of my regular classes. That part's no sweat."

"Conte, wait. Wait." Greg shook his head, as if he'd just awakened. "What do you do with the fourteen minutes you saved?" He leered, fishlike. "Build a rocket?"

"I'll do homework," Conte said scornfully. "Listen, I'm not just trying to get a bunch of marks on paper. When I graduate, I'm really gonna know things. Those HIC classes don't mean that I won't have to study. The only difference is that I don't have to attend regular classes."

Greg looked skeptical, rubbing his nose, but he said nothing.

"Third period," Conte continued, "I pull the same kind of switch. *Mark Conte* goes to regular biology with Mr. Dean. I take English as a HIC course. Fourth period, I go to band. The art class for *Mark Conte* is all independent study. We work on our own time, at our own pace, and turn in the projects when they're due. Fifth period, as you can see," he said with a flourish of the pointer, "I go to Miss Merriman's regular algebra class, taking HIC history, and last I have English and HIC biology. Thus, I attend six classes like everybody else. I sandwich in six more, plus Early Bird P.E."

Greg opened one eye wearily. Like a tired old man, his head had begun to bob down on his chest. "How do you fit in homework for twelve different classes?"

"Combine and conquer," said Conte. "That's how. I knew a guy in Texas who used the same project for four different classes. When he got done, he gave it to his neighbor. The neighbor sold it to another kid. Altogether, that project must have been used a dozen times."

"What was it?"

"A model of a guillotine," Conte replied. "It was made of toothpicks and wires. They used it for an art project first. One guy used it as a special project for his literature class, when they were reading *A Tale of Two Cities*. Then, of course, it was perfect for history."

"I see what you mean," Greg said, nodding. "You can probably get English credit for your biology project. You could do a report on some famous scientist. Use the same report for both classes."

They were both silent for a few minutes, contemplating the range of possibilities. Then Greg asked, "Conte, what are you going to do when you graduate two years from now? You'll only be sixteen."

"Oh, I guess I'll go to the University of Chicago," Conte said casually.

"But Conte, will you really know enough?"

"Of course I will!" Conte exclaimed. But that small inner voice screamed out, *Will you? Will you?* "Of course I'll be ready for college," he persisted. "Anyhow, I plan to really do a lot of extra work. Like algebra. I'll work ahead and do a whole year's work in one semester. Then I can take the qualifying exam to get into geometry later this year. Oh, I'll be ready for college."

They went upstairs, where Mrs. Gaff stood bent over a large fish tank. Slowly she straightened up, moved toward them and said in her whispery voice, "Hello, Conte. I understand you boys are going to take up fencing. Let me know," she said with a gasp, "perhaps I can use some."

The boys walked to the door. Hesitantly Conte asked, "What did your mother mean?"

Greg shrugged. "Who knows?"

It was clear that Mrs. Gaff never really listened, so absorbed was she in the silent world of her fishes. No wonder Greg repeats himself, Conte thought. He almost started to say something sympathetic, then retreated into a businesslike tone.

"I'll need to get approval from Mr. Rhinefinger and Miss Worfenstein to take HIC courses," he said. "What are they like?"

"I've never had either of them," Greg replied. Suddenly he seemed apprehensive. He glanced over his shoulder toward his mother, who still stood hunched over in the shadows. "I don't know, Conte," he said. "Maybe we'd better just forget it, call it quits, end this thing before there's trouble. I don't want to get involved in any trouble . . ."

"OK," said Conte. "I'll handle it. I know where to get the information I need."

Fortunately, he had kept his ear to the ground, so to speak. He'd heard plenty of kids yelling at each other, "See you at Katz!" All through the day kids roared down the hill beyond the cliffs at the edge of town down to the seashore. They came in cars, on bikes, on skate boards, and on foot.

"See you at Katz." "You gonna be at Katz today?" "Party at Katz tonight!" That's how it went. By his second week in Vista Mar, Conte had decided to find out what all the fuss was about. He had asked directions from the high school boy who worked at a nearby gas station.

"Katz? Yeah, that's where all the action is, man. You never been there? Oh, you're new. Well, go down by the high school, then you can either slide down the cliffs or take the path a little further down. Why they call it Katz? I dunno."

But the old man at the Stop and Shop Grocery knew. And he had been delighted to tell it.

"Years ago," he said in his high pitched, nasal twang, "there was a passel of wild cats down there at the beach. Not real wild cats, mind you, but cats that people wanted to get rid of. They'd set 'em out there by the cliffs, and pretty soon they went wild living there on the beach. Guess they lived on rats and mice and sand crabs. So all night you'd hear a terrible racket from the beach, yeowling and caterwauling. People started callin' it the Katzenjammer Beach. Like that cartoon, you know, the Katzenjammer Kids. Then kids from the high school started going down there. 'Cause of the name, I guess. So, of course with the kids howling and yeowling and carrying on down there, people still called it Katzenjammer Beach. Time went by. The cats disappeared. But the name stuck. The kids shortened it to Katz."

The next morning, Friday, Conte set off for Katz.

5   Available
Worfenstein
Is and Isn't

When Conte got to Katz Beach, things were in full swing. It was a place of endless fascination—a place which, according to the adults in the community, no person in his right mind would care to spend more than ten minutes at. That in itself made it doubly attractive to kids. They were drawn to it like flies to a rotting carcass.

Picture a dirty ribbon of sand. Behind it loom jutting cliffs encrusted with gray scrub brush. Before it beckons the wide Pacific. But in this hapless spot, that beautiful ocean slaps against nature's garbage dump: the shore is littered with rocks. Huge, flat rocks. Small spikey rocks —a person could make a fortune selling Band-Aids at Katz Beach. Between the rocks, huge beetle-eyed and crunchy crabs show their ugly faces. Squashed beer cans, broken pop bottles and a confetti of gum and candy wrappers make this a collector's paradise, an ecologist's nightmare. This, then, is Katz Beach.

From the first time he saw it, Conte had had a certain feeling about Katz Beach. He loved it absolutely. Here a guy could lie on his belly in the sand or bob on a rubber raft and watch a continually passing parade of girls in bikinis. And by intuition Conte had known from that very first visit that Katz Beach was the cradle of all pertinent information about Vista Mar's teen population.

How did he know it? He knew, because of having lived in four different towns. Every town has its *place*, be it the local PO, the drive-in restaurant, the library, or even a certain used car lot. How do you recognize the *place*? Well, if you don't know it when you see it, and when you *hear* it, forget it.

At Katz Beach everyone came alive. The girls seemed to glitter. The guys were always laughing. Jokes came out funnier at Katz Beach. The air was cool or warm, depending upon what you needed. And the music at Katz Beach! Music all day long, from guitars, from wooden flutes, from tiny transistor radios, from four girls harmonizing, from three guys playing the bongos. Music all day long, and every moment the scene changed like a larger-than-life kaleidescope, with people coming, other people leaving, walking, running, swimming, *moving*.

Conte sauntered down to Katz Beach. And by some

miracle (inwardly he sang grateful praises!) he saw Pamela Patterson. She was walking with two other girls. All three were wearing bikinis. He walked. He walked straight past them. He turned. Thank God! Pamela had turned, too. He began to grin, walking backwards away from her. He spun, walked backwards toward her, and the girls set up a trilling giggle, a silly flittering flirting— they sat down on the sand. Conte and Pamela Patterson and Mary in the orange bikini and Mary Lou in lavender. All morning, while they drank eleven strawberry sodas between them, Conte felt like the funniest man on earth. Pamela, Mary, and Mary Lou laughed at nearly everything he said. Mary and Mary Lou, being sophomores, supplied him with the following information:

1. Available Worfenstein was usually not available.
2. However, she could often be found loitering around the band room or the office or any place where Mr. Mott, the music teacher, might be found.
3. She believed that she was very sexy.

About Mr. Rhinefinger, Conte learned the following:

1. He was an ecology nut.
2. His son, now in college, had once flunked out of a private school.
3. Rhinefinger believed there was a conspiracy be-

tween private schools and "those crackpots in Washington" to hound him out of his job.

Armed with this information, Conte telephoned the school that afternoon to make an appointment first with Mr. Rhinefinger, then with Miss Worfenstein. At Rhinefinger's office he gave his name as Mark Conte. The lie didn't hurt a bit. No small voice screamed out at him. In fact, nothing bothered him at all. The magic of Katz Beach had worked its way into his total being. Life was beautiful, and for more reasons than one.

Just before they left the beach, Mary and Mary Lou had suddenly gotten lost or evaporated, and Conte and Pamela had taken a walk. They had wandered up the gentle mound at the bottom of the cliff to a place where a strange tree grew. It stuck straight out from the side of the cliff, hanging out almost parallel to the ground. But stranger still were the slips of paper fastened to it, rippling and fluttering in the breeze. Conte had not noticed it before.

"What's this?" Conte pointed.

"Messages," said Pamela.

"For whom?"

"Oh, for anybody. See, it's like the Want Ads in the paper."

Yes, there was one about Irish setter pups for sale. Another advertised for a lost bike. Little notes were tied on with string or rubber bands, or they were merely thrust into the branches. A few of the messages were obscene. But most were legitimate, and Conte was impressed. This tree with its dangling messages—this was terrific. To his utter amazement, someone had stuck a small note into the bark with a safety pin, proclaiming, "ROB OWENS IS TAKING EARLY BIRD P.E."

For the second time since moving to Vista Mar (the first being his discovery of Katz Beach), Conte felt jubilant. Maybe Vista Mar wasn't going to be so bad, after all. Looking further, he saw all sorts of personal messages, declarations of love, private jokes, general announcements. He could begin to imagine many possibilities for this tree, yes indeed. For now, he took a gum wrapper from his pocket, found a stub of pencil and wrote, "THE MARK HAS ARRIVED."

School began the following Monday. It was four days before Conte could see Mr. Rhinefinger—four days of total chaos.

Vista Mar High School was like a town under siege. This spirit of battle would continue for three full weeks, until the students had accustomed themselves to their new classes, making changes in their schedules and in general creating such commotion that experienced teachers just lay low and waited for the dust to settle.

The office was packed, steaming, alive with noise and

motion on Thursday morning when Conte went to see Mr. Rhinefinger. He had rehearsed this session well before the mirror the night before. Everything depended upon Rhinefinger's approval of two HIC classes and the special project art class.

Conte knocked. Mr. Rhinefinger appeared immediately, hustled Conte inside, then proceeded to peer outside his door both ways, then hastily close it again. For several moments the counselor sat behind his desk, head cocked as if listening for some hidden electronic device. At last he checked the calendar on his desk and said, as if affirming the fact, "Mark Conte."

"Yes sir." Conte handed him the schedule for *Mark Conte*, #3449. "I'm signed up for music," he explained, "but I'd like to take special project art with Mr. Stanley. See, it says here in the bulletin . . ."

"But Mark, that course is for advanced students."

"I am advanced, sir. Since my mother is an artist, I was—er, born with a paint brush in my hand, you might say."

Mr. Rhinefinger frowned and glanced over his shoulder. Secretively he said, "If it were up to me, Mark, there would be no problem. But there are—ah—certain elements that would like to see me falter, yes, that would even want to take my job . . ."

Conte made himself think of tragic things, until he was certain his expression had been molded into what his mom called, "that hangdog, hound dog look." He nodded dejectedly and said, "I guess my mother was right."

"Well, now, don't take it so hard, Mark. Maybe you can take the special art class next year."

"By next year," said Conte with a shrug, "who knows? I already had a project in mind, too. But my mom warned me. 'You can't get individual training in the public schools,' she told me."

Conte stood up, as if to leave. He smiled sadly at Mr. Rhinefinger. "I argued with her. I told her I'd be able to take special classes through the HIC program. I have been a HIC for years. I told my mother that at Vista Mar the curriculum would be *flexible*." He sighed deeply. "She told me to forget it and apply to Brockhaven, which is kind of expensive, but my mom thinks it's worth it."

"Mark!" Rhinefinger rose off his chair in alarm. "I would think twice—oh, more than twice, before considering such a step. *Brockhaven!*" All his features contracted, as if he had bitten into a very sour fruit.

"I've heard Brockhaven is a good school, sir. I've heard that at Brockhaven a person can study at his own pace and do special projects, like that art project I want to do. It's based on an ecology theme."

For a long, agonizing moment Conte felt that this time he had gone too far. He felt hot and itchy, as if suddenly his skin had grown too tight. Those awful lies! He caught childhood visions of Pinocchio, and unwittingly Conte felt for his nose.

"Ecology," said Mr. Rhinefinger with emphasis, "happens to be a special interest of mine. Last year I marched with the Citizens for a Cleaner Environment."

"I read about that march in the newspaper!" Conte exclaimed. That, at least, was true. What Conte failed to mention was that the article had been quite derogatory. The marchers had left behind so much litter that it took city workers three days to sweep up.

Mr. Rhinefinger pressed his fingertips together. "I suppose we could make an exception, in view of the fact that your mother is an artist. And since you are a HIC. Here at Vista Mar High," he said grandly, "we fit the program to the individual, not the other way around."

His telephone rang. He snatched it up. "What? Oh, Davis. You don't want to take art appreciation? You had it last year in New York? Never mind, Davis. Take it again. You know every sophomore has to take art appreciation. Play by the rules, Davis!"

Mr. Rhinefinger turned back to Conte. He scribbled a note. "Give this to Mr. Stanley for the art class. As for the HIC courses, you may take two of them. Just find yourself a faculty sponsor for each, and let me know the name. Of course, you understand that you'll be responsible for the state-required curriculum. You and your

HIC sponsor will work out what aspects of the course you will pursue in greater depth. Good luck to you, Mark. Let me see your art project when it's finished."

Having left Mr. Rhinefinger's office, Conte felt strangely dejected. He should have been happy. Instead he had a nagging sensation of guilt, rather like a tooth-ache.

"Where can I find Miss Worfenstein?" he asked the office secretary.

"Out back. T 27."

"T?"

"Temporary shack," she replied. "Huh. Built thirty years ago, during the war. That's how temporary."

Conte found the row of shacks beyond the regular buildings. Inside the dim and dingy room stood a desk and two chairs. On the desk was a note, "Out to Lunch." It was ten-thirty. Obviously, Miss Worfenstein was not available.

Near noon Miss Worfenstein arrived. She met him at the door of the shack, beaming.

There was this aspect of beaming about her, caused probably by the peculiar style of her hair. Shades of blond, it ranged from beige to dull gold with several colors in between. All around her head the hair stood straight out, about two inches long, like the feathery rays of an Indian headdress.

The uniqueness of Miss Worfenstein lay not only in

the cut of her hair, but also in her voice. She warbled. Once you heard the laugh of Worfenstein, you never forgot. Conte, a musician of some experience, immediately realized that the laugh of Worfenstein began at high *D* and descended in a five note arpeggio.

She seemed pleasant. "Conte? Conte Mark?" she said. "An unusual name, isn't it—oo-whoo-whoo-whoo-whoo!"

"My mom named me after Richard Conte, the actor," he explained. "It's an unusual first name, but then, my mom is an unusual person."

That brought another trill. Then they got down to business. Yes, Miss Worfenstein was glad to approve Early Bird P.E., fencing. She agreed that it would be a good idea for him to take study hall for first period. As to taking HIC English, Miss Worfenstein had a good suggestion. "Mr. Gireaux is a good teacher," she said. "You will know him from your fencing class. Perhaps he will sponsor you for English. I could telephone him for you," she suggested, "and ask him."

Conte nodded. "I'd appreciate that," he said.

From her desk drawer Miss Worfenstein took out a little black book, dialed a number and identified herself, "Oscar? This is Mildred. Mildred who? Why, you'll have to guess—oo-whoo-whoo-whoo-whoo!"

By the end of their meeting four things were settled. Miss Worfenstein had a tennis date with Mr. Gireaux for Saturday morning. Mr. Gireaux agreed to be Conte's supervisor for HIC English. Miss Worfenstein herself decided to sponsor Conte for HIC biology. (She would teach him a thing or two—oo-whoo-whoo-whoo-*whoo*!) And lastly, Miss Worfenstein would personally see Mr. Mott about getting Conte into the band.

Conte objected, "But I'm already signed up."

"Take nothing for granted," she snapped, and whipped out her sign that said, "Out to Lunch."

Conte asked, "When should I report to you for biology?"

"Weekly," she said, "once or twice. Anytime of day. I am always . . ." she hurried to the door, let him out, slammed it shut. ". . . always available."

6 Back To Katz

Registration time at Vista Mar High had once meant total uproar. Students were assigned to the wrong classes. Lines stretched from the office all the way to the cafeteria. It took weeks to get everything straightened out.

Then came Mr. Gordon Kelly and the computer. Registration was *still* chaos. Students were *still* assigned to the wrong classes. The line stretched from the office all the way to the cafeteria, around the gym and back again. But now it was only a question of "slight mechanical malfunction," and Mr. Granberg, the principal, felt secure. He believed in the inherent perfection of the machine and in the devotion of its keeper, Mr. Gordon Kelly.

Some people said that Mr. Gordon Kelly had a pet name for the computer. Pu, as in "pew." Some said he actually spoke to it. "Pu, why did you put forty freshman girls into senior physics instead of sewing I-A?

Pu, you gave some students three lunch periods, while others got none. Oh, Pu," he lamented, "how can you confuse varsity football with modern dance?"

Poor Mr. Gordon Kelly had nightmares wherein the top of his head opened up like a lid and a truck dumped a load of garbage inside. The dream had its basis in a common saying among computer professionals: garbage in—garbage out.

Naturally, when something went wrong, Mr. Kelly felt guilty. He felt that he must have put garbage in to have gotten garbage out. And if he put garbage in, why, there must be garbage *inside his brain*. So every October Mr. Kelly had to take a leave of absence because of nervous tension. His doctor did not call it that. He called it "interior circuit overload."

It was important for Conte to note that each semester Mr. Kelly accepted a chosen few students into his special class called computer science. Conte would not need to take this class until next year. But he filed the information in his mind, just as he began immediately to file the idiosyncrasies of his various teachers. As the son of a psychologist, he knew that life was easier when you psyched people out.

By the beginning of the second week of school Conte's program was already taking shape. The Early Bird fencing class was fabulous. With so many students enrolled, it would take weeks for Mr. Gireaux to sort out the names and faces. As for faces—the fencing mask would help considerably to keep Conte anonymous.

Just as he'd thought, the study hall teacher only asked that they sign in. Immediately after the bell she disappeared, destined for the teacher's lounge to have a smoke.

Coach Brown, it is true, began to recognize Conte by his stroke—and also by the fact that he was the only student ready to swim fourteen minutes before time. During those minutes Conte would sit on the bleachers reading his history assignment for Miss Sommers.

Miss Sommers, sweet and naïve, was game to swallow any story, no matter how strange. Each year the graduating seniors voted her as the teacher who was "the most sincere." Conte felt truly sorry every time he had to lie to her.

Why would he lie to a sincere teacher like Miss Sommers? Because—ah, the rub—he could not get an HIC algebra class.

During the whole second week of school Conte tried to fight the policy. He badgered Mr. Rhinefinger. He hinted at FBI investigations and an international conspiracy of private school teachers who sent detectives to spy on high school counselors who did not comply with the state law regarding HICs. No dice. School policy, repeated in capital letters, was: NO STUDENT IS ALLOWED TO TAKE ALGEBRA AS A HIC COURSE.

What to do? What to do?

Miss Merriman had a monopoly on teaching algebra. In fact, that's all she taught.

Why not have one of him take a different math course?

No way. Every college bound freshman had to take algebra, and Conte hadn't had it in eighth grade. Algebra was a prerequisite for all other math courses. So, Conte decided to use his wits—and his feet.

As *Mark Conte* he reported to second period algebra and subtly urged Miss Merriman to hurry and take roll by crying out, "Here comes the monitor from the office to pick up the attendance sheet!"

He sat in the back of the room near the door; after shouting "Here!" he would slip out and run to the history building. His goal was to arrive and yell out "Here!" just when Miss Sommers got to the M's and called, "Conte Mark."

It often worked. When it didn't, Conte had to offer one of a long list of excuses. "I had a nosebleed." Then something more dramatic, like the suspicion that he was coming down with leprosy and needed to see the school nurse.

Miss Sommers wrinkled her brow, evidently concerned that one so young was already a confirmed hypochondriac. But she let it pass.

Fourth period was a cinch. Conte went to band, since

his corresponding art class was truly "self-directed." The first project, a mixed media presentation, was not due until December 3.

Fifth period Conte went to Miss Merriman's algebra class and usually stayed there. Once a week or so he spent a few minutes with his HIC history teacher, Mr. Morse, who simply told Conte to read the text, to be thinking about a project, and to start reading a dozen extra books from a prepared reading list. No sweat. Conte had already decided to switch from showers to baths. He could read while soaking. Amazing how much time one could save when one paid attention to details.

Sixth period English with Mrs. Aherne was the usual stuff—parts of speech, spelling, book reports. Simple. He'd use some of the same books as for history. As for his HIC biology class with Miss Worfenstein—well, she had not yet made herself available to Conte to discuss a project. So he just drifted along, studying regular biology with Mr. Dean during third period. He had already paved the way with Mr. Dean for getting extra credit for the HIC biology project he would be doing anyhow for Miss Worfenstein. Clever.

If he was so clever, Conte wondered near the end of the second week, why was he always so exhausted? Sometimes he fell asleep standing propped up against the refrigerator, an open carton of milk in his hand. Sometimes his mind felt fuzzy and befuddled, so that he failed to recognize people—namely his dad when the latter came peeking into Conte's bedroom one evening and Conte screamed out in fright.

On Saturday morning after the first two weeks of school Conte managed to find time to get on the bathroom scale. He discovered that he had lost five pounds.

From running? Maybe. Or maybe it was from his new dietary habits. He often missed lunch, spending that time explaining his absence or tardiness to one of his teachers. His dinners were not very tasty. Whenever possible he tossed his food into the blender and drank it. Surprising how much time was saved by not having to chew.

He assured his mother that it was a new Oriental technique, advocated by many gurus. His mom looked skeptical, but she did not interfere. How could she? Anyone who had once been on a two-week diet of dates, seaweed, and soy nuts was hardly in a position to lecture about nutrition.

By the third week of school it became clear to Conte that he couldn't keep up the pace. After fencing and swimming, the daily rush between algebra and history was getting him down. As he sat in class whispering to Pamela one morning, he suddenly discovered a way out of his dilemma.

Miss Merriman, squinting at him and Pamela, called

out, "Quiet! You, the girl with the medallion around her neck, *pay attention*!"

She squinted around the room, her lips sternly pursed, then continued, "Problem number three—you. The boy with the leather jacket."

That evening Conte approached Greg Gaff for a loan. Greg was less than eager to get into high finance. "Why do you need a buck ninety-eight? How will that get you out of algebra?"

"Actually, I need $2.10. With tax." Conte patted his pockets. "I'm broke. I had to send my five bucks to that Comminger Catalogue Company. They were threatening me with legal action again. I owed them for an old-fashioned phone I bought last summer."

"You still got the phone?" Greg perked up.

"Sure," Conte said. "I've got it hooked up to my stereo. When the phone rings, it activates the stereo—instead of hello you get rock music."

"Bring it over here," Greg said, suddenly tough.

"Why? What do you mean? I told you, it's hooked up . . ."

"I'll keep it in hock," Greg said firmly, "until you pay me back the $2.10. Business is business. And if you don't mind my asking, I'd like to know exactly what you intend to do with my money."

"I'm going to the sporting goods store tomorrow to buy myself a ski cap. Green."

"And that will help you with your problems with Miss Merriman?"

"Yep. That, and a visit to the hanging tree at Katz."

"What in the world is a hanging tree?"

"Are you kidding? Don't you ever go to Katz?"

"Never," Greg said. "I've got enough fish and sea water here at home. I hate fish. So do my brothers."

"I didn't know you had any . . ."

"They're both away. One's at college. The other works in Michigan. We all hate fish. Which doesn't mean we hate my mother!" He looked tough again. "She's always left us pretty much alone, as long as we let her tend her fishes. They're her thing, her life, her hobby, her obsession. You know, her *career*."

"Greg," began Conte, "did you ever notice that you have a habit of repeating everything?"

"No. Never, not at all. I don't."

"I don't mean repeating exactly—but you say the same thing in so many different ways . . . well, never mind."

Whispering in class, Conte invited Pamela to go down to the beach with him after school. Pamela nodded and smiled.

Katz Beach was different now that school had begun. Only a few avid surfers came there in the afternoon.

Conte and Pamela sauntered back and forth, back and

forth along the strip of beach. The cliffs rising behind them seemed less barren now. Was it possible that a new kind of moss had grown to soften the rocks? The scrub brush seemed less scrubby. Conte took Pamela's hand. They spoke about many things.

Pamela had a problem. Intently Conte listened while she explained. "I want to be in the band," she said, "instead of in music appreciation." She crinkled her nose in distaste. Everybody hated music appreciation. "I play the flute. But I heard that band members have to be in the marching band, too."

"True. We march during half time at the football games, and in competition against other schools." Conte's thinking was already far, far ahead. He envisioned himself with Pamela, riding the bus to far away places, marching in parades, eating lunch together on the lawn . . .

"I'd love to be in the marching band," she said sadly, "but I could never do it. Never in a million years."

"Don't you play the flute well enough?"

"Oh, I'm good on the flute!" Pamela said. "It's just that I can't—I never could—I don't know my right hand from my left," she confessed.

Conte frowned and pursed his lips. "Are you putting me on?"

"No. It's true. I must have a mental block or something."

"Well, what hand do you write with? That ought to help."

"No," Pamela said gloomily. "I'm ambidextrous."

"Listen," Conte said excitedly, "don't worry about it at all. You just get your counselor to give you band, and I'll take care of everything. When we march, the flutes come right behind the saxophones. So all you have to do is watch me and follow me. Besides," he said, "Mr. Mott needs another flute player in the band, and that's a fact. He'd love to have you."

The fact was that Mr. Mott's band needed another flute player the way a dog needs fleas. But Conte would work it out. Already he was on good terms with Mr. Mott. All he had to do was to come to some kind of agreement with Charlotta Jones—or to edge her out. He'd do a few favors for Mr. Mott, have a persuasive chat. . . .

Although Pamela didn't know her right hand from her left, Conte discovered that she was really smart. She, too, was a HIC. Conte was amazed. They had so much in common. Except for one thing. Conte got the impression that she was scrupulously honest.

He decided to have it out, here and now, and so he asked her, "Pamela, if a person did something that another person thought was strange or even dishonest, do you think that other person would be mad at the person even if they didn't know why the person was doing it?"

"No," said Pamela.

"Well, that's good," sighed Conte. He took out a note from his pocket, and a small thumb tack. He proceeded to tack the note to the trunk of the hanging tree. The note said, "PERSON IN MERRIMAN'S 2ND PER. ALGEBRA NEEDS BOY TO DO SIMPLE FAVOR IN EXCHANGE FOR SAME. CALL 388-4291. C. MARK."

Pamela wisely asked no questions, but she said, "Have you noticed how Miss Merriman never calls people by their right names?"

"I've noticed," said Conte.

"Like, she calls me 'the girl with the medallion,' and she calls Peggy Wirts 'the girl with the braids,' and Stu Robbins is 'the boy in the army jacket.' Do you think she knows our names at all?"

"I hope not," said Conte.

"Where are we going now?" Pamela asked.

"To the sporting goods store."

"What for?"

"To buy me a ski cap. Bright green."

7 She Was
a Nice Girl, But ...

When Conte had first seen Charlotta Jones, he had wondered what all the fuss was about. She wasn't gorgeous. She wasn't the school celebrity. But everybody in the music department, and especially the boys in the band, spoke of her often and always with a certain gleam in their eyes.

Just why Charlotta was even enrolled in band was a mystery. She played no musical instrument. She had no musical background whatsoever. But Charlotta could be found in the band room nearly any time of day, shuffling music, running errands for Mr. Mott, looking busy but never really doing much. Or she might just be perched on one of the stools, staring into space, fiddling with her hair or filing her nails.

Perhaps the school officials, sensing that Charlotta Jones needed a home away from home, simply looked the other way. Or perhaps, officially, Charlotta never existed at all. She was just one of those people who manage to drift through high school without suffering the inconvenience of studying or attending classes.

Conte, of course, had met Charlotta during the first week of school. She was obviously, though unofficially, the band manager. It was a position that Conte had held before, in eighth grade, and one he now coveted. How had Charlotta, with no musical talent, risen to such heights? Conte had soon learned the facts:

Charlotta was now a junior. During her freshman and sophomore years, Charlotta Jones had achieved a measure of fame, particularly with the boys in the band. She had a reputation for being—well, friendly. So filled was Charlotta with brotherly love, and so fair in dispensing her favor, that word got around fast.

Charlotta was very busy. Her rendezvous included stolen moments between classes, trysts before and after school, meetings during lunch hour. She was, as the fellows said, "a nice girl, but—too generous."

Charlotta did have a particular love for musicians, and many of her "friends" were band members. Thus, they made her first mascot, then band manager. Mr. Mott, a placid and sweetly unsuspecting sort, felt sorry for the girl and let her hang around. It did not occur to him to wonder exactly how the morale of the band had come to be boosted one hundred percent by her presence.

Now all that was changed. Sometime during the summer, Charlotta Jones had reformed. The word was that for the first time in her life, Charlotta had "got religion."

Some said she just got tired of her hectic life. But most of the kids agreed that sometime in June, Charlotta had been seen at a tent revival meeting over in the next town of Arlington Hills. Since that night, they said, Charlotta had remained pure.

The trouble was, Charlotta had gotten into the habit of being generous and she couldn't simply walk away from all her friends, especially the boys in the band. So she did what any smart, reformed sinner would do. She substituted one manner of giving for another. By the end of the first week in school every student in the music department knew that if anybody needed a written excuse for tardiness or absence, Charlotta Jones would be happy to supply it.

She was good at it, too. She could sign a dozen different signatures, and she brought to her new service the flair and imagination of a politician or a comedy writer.

Her notes could be beautifully simple:

Ronnie Myers was absent yesterday because he was sick.

> Sincerely,
> Alma Myers

If the occasion demanded it, the notes could be ingeniously complex:

> Joe Tammaran was late this morning because he had an accident at home. While teetering in his chair at breakfast, Joe fell back and smashed the patio window. The cat jumped out through the window and suffered cuts and lacerations. Joe is tardy because he had to take the cat to the vet.
>
> Sincerely,
> Bonnie Tammaran
>
> P.S. Joe is going to have to pay for the broken window. If you know of any jobs for students, please advise. Joe is a good worker, reliable and cautious. B.T.

The moment Conte first saw Charlotta Jones, he knew that she knew that he knew: they were destined to become rivals.

Rivals for what?

For control of the band.

But wasn't control of the band the prerogative of the music teacher, Mr. Mott? Maybe. Maybe not.

One look at the band room with its hopeless clutter, its instrument cases stacked dangerously in the aisles, sheet music strewn about like autumn leaves in a storm —one look at the percussion instruments thrown into a jumbled heap on top of the dust-laden piano, at the blackboards criss-crossed with messages—one peek into the tiny office room adjoining the classroom, that office with its bulging bookcases and stuffed file cabinets, a desk, a chair, and room for two persons at most, where on the wall a huge poster proclaimed "Maximum capacity of this room is 500 persons!"—one look at all this, and Conte knew the band had to be his baby. It *had* to be.

It was in seventh grade, under the guidance of Mr. Birdie, that Conte had grown to love a band. It wasn't that he *loved* the music or the teacher or the group. No —although all these were part of it—his real love was just for all the stuff, noise, confusion, vibrations, the very *atmosphere* of the band.

At graduation from intermediate school, Conte had won the Student Achievement Award for Music. Conte's mother, dabbing at her eyes, had muttered, "I guess Mr. Birdie's glad to see you graduate. I guess he'll be glad to get his band back again. You really pulled it out from under him, didn't you?" She glared at him as was her way, and Conte played along, pretending not to know that she was crying because he was going into high school, which meant he wasn't her baby anymore, which meant *she* was getting older too. And more tears and fierce looks, because she was so proud he'd won the award. Oh, his mother was very emotional, but she'd never admit it. So he glared back at her and said, "Yeah, and I'll be glad to get away from this dumb band."

His award was a trophy about thirty inches tall. Conte kept it in the corner behind his door. Usually he hung his cap on it, or threw his old sweatshirt over it. Occasionally the door banged into it and it fell over. Conte didn't care. Just once in a while, late at night and in secret, he would lovingly polish his trophy with a little rag he kept under his mattress, using spit and a speck of toothpaste. The night after he first met Charlotta Jones, he had sat up late polishing and spitting and polishing.

He had felt awful. He was nobody. And Charlotta's control of the band was secure. He'd thought—he'd hoped—no. It was not possible. There were sixty kids in the band, all bigger, better, more popular than Conte. Where was his place? If he were an athlete, he'd have a team, buddies, practice sessions. But he was too short for basketball, too chicken for football, too clumsy for baseball. As for swimming, he could manage if he kept moving. Heaven forbid, he should try to float; he sank like a lead weight clear to the bottom. And, unlike most sinkers, Conte only came up twice. So much for the swimming team. Unless he distinguished himself in the band, he was nowhere. He was nobody.

On Wednesday of the third week of school, he wasn't exactly a nobody anymore. In second period algebra he became known as "the boy with the green ski cap."

Now all he needed was for somebody else to wear that cap during roll call and for an occasional recitation. Thus far, his message left on the hanging tree at Katz remained unanswered.

In fifth period algebra, he wore a pair of wraparound sunglasses, and became known accordingly as "the boy with the big shades."

In this third week of school, a general restlessness and nervousness seemed to seize the students. The end had come. They were stuck in their schedules with no escape for the rest of the semester. Conte assured Pamela that Mr. Mott would, before the end of the week, be requesting her participation in the band. But when Conte mentioned it, Mr. Mott got a vague and misty look about the eyes. Obviously, he couldn't say yes and hated to say no.

To Conte's astonishment, into the band on that third week came a new piccolo player, burly and amber-eyed —Kurt Zelinkowitz.

"Where's my five bucks?" Conte demanded, glaring.

Charlotta Jones appeared immediately at Kurt's elbow. Obviously, she also considered herself as mediator of all disputes in the band room. She asked, "How come he owes you five bucks?"

Conte explained about the wager at the freshman orientation.

Now Charlotta turned to Zelinkowitz, whose great bulk seemed to shrink before the girl's scrutiny. His amber eyes flickered uneasily. Sheepishly he admitted, "I did run out on him, but it was a dumb bet. Just because he's got that dumb name."

"What dumb name?" Conte cried. "Look at your name."

No wonder he couldn't stand it in high school, with these immature juveniles and their stupid arguments. Oh, he couldn't wait to get out of here and into university, with decent people who could discuss things in a sane manner . . .

"Zelinkowitz," he yelled, "if you don't give me my five bucks, I'm gonna ram that piccolo down your . . ."

"Cut it out," said Charlotta, without raising her voice. To Zelinkowitz she said, "What were you doing at the freshman orientation, anyway?"

"Just wanted to look around," Kurt mumbled. "Gee, Charlotta, I didn't mean anything. I just . . ."

"Pay him the five bucks," she said.

"I spent it."

"Pay him."

"Gee, Charlotta, I ain't got that kind of money anymore. You know we haven't done anything to make that kind of dough . . ."

"Shut up, Zelinkowitz," said Charlotta calmly. She turned to Conte. "I go down to the beach at Katz," she said. "I happen to know you need a favor. Maybe we can arrange something."

"Maybe," said Conte. He tightened his lips and spoke out of the corner of his mouth. "But that's just a small thing. It ain't worth the whole five bucks."

"You want something else?"

Conte nodded. He held his breath, made himself speak slowly and with a slight drawl, opening his mouth just a crack. "There is a little something you could do for me. There's this chick that plays the flute," he said with a casual shrug. "I told her I'd help her get into the band. She needs Mr. Mott's permission."

"No sweat," said Charlotta Jones.

"I've mentioned it to him," added Conte. "Mr. Mott seems to think he's got enough flute players."

"The Lord," said Charlotta, "works in mysterious ways."

It was indeed mysterious. On Friday of the third week of school one of the flute players came down with a horrible case of strep throat. A second flute player was temporarily out of commission; her instrument, bent like a pretzel, would take several weeks to repair. Another flute player undertook a thorough and systematic search —high, low and in between. Her instrument had vanished.

In succeeding years this day would be known as the

"Curse of the Flutes." Mr. Mott, flustered and twitching, gratefully admitted Pamela Patterson, flute player *with whole instrument*, into the band.

Conte was astounded, awed and scared. He had seldom witnessed such wielding of power. And the next night he received a mysterious phone call.

"Understand ya need a little favor in algebra, second period. You gonna be home tomorrow? We'll be over to discuss your proposition."

"Who is this?" Conte asked, "Who is this?"

"The name's Flint. Wayne Flint."

Next Conte heard the harsh sound of the dial tone, and he shuddered. Greg had warned him. "Stay away from Flint—Flint the Fence, they call him." Greg didn't know why he was called that, but the name sounded ominous.

Suddenly Conte's mother appeared at his side. She was grinning with delight. "A new friend?" she inquired. "Coming over tomorrow?"

"You were listening on the extension!" he accused.

"I couldn't help it," she said. "The phone was off the hook in my garret."

She called it "the garret," the little room where she'd installed a workbench and shelves, and where she pounded out her STATEMENTS from metal odds and ends.

"He's not a friend," Conte grumbled.

"Well, you be sure to invite him in," she said, looking smug. "I bought a six-pack of root beer today, just in case."

That night Conte slept badly. In his dreams, Flint the Fence had a knife blade face. He was dressed all in black leather, chasing Pamela Patterson up and down the cliffs at Katz. In accompaniment to Conte's dreams, Dag, for reasons of his own, set up a mournful howling.

Conte's dream changed. He stood in the middle of a football field, wearing a tall beaver hat. Surrounding him were six different high school bands, sporting their distinctive colors. Banners waved. People cheered. Conte mounted the dais. Over the microphone came the announcement, "The Vista Mar student conductor, Conte Mark! Mark Conte! Conte Mark!"

His names rang out in great echoes as he lifted his baton and snapped it smartly through the air. He tapped his foot, cued in the trumpets, prolonged the drum roll, brought them all together to a crescendo. He was in control. All eyes were upon him. But suddenly the trumpets, clarinets, saxophones and French horns combined into a doleful chorus of howls. Musicians dropped their instruments, and as they maliciously pursued him, all were transformed into a pack of wildly howling mad dogs.

It was sunny and quiet that Sunday afternoon. Bad dreams forgotten, a certain sleepiness remained, and

Conte had spent the last hour or so working on his art project. He would create a terrific multi-media sculpture. He would use the sand and driftwood and scrub brush he'd brought from the beach, along with other odds and ends. Perhaps he'd call it "Crisis at Sea," or "Evolution of Fishes."

Conte congratulated himself on planning ahead. He was making good use of his time. By using natural objects, he could work in a scientific theme and use the project for HIC biology as well as art. Perhaps he'd make an explanatory poster or written statement and get English credit, too.

He lay down on the grass, feeling totally relaxed and very pleased. To survive, to triumph was really so simple once one began to organize one's thoughts. How wonderful it was, he mused, to be totally in command of your own destiny.

So sweet was his reverie that he forgot he'd left the gate open while he was lugging his stuff into the yard. But Dag, the Great Dane, remembered.

One moment Conte was snoozing in the sun. The next moment he heard a scream, a thud, curses, shouts, and commotion. When he got out to the street, there stood Dennis Downer and Kurt Zelinkowitz, bent over their buddy who was stretched out flat on the sidewalk—that buddy who, Conte knew, could be none other than Flint the Fence.

Conte's dad kept trying to straddle the dog. Dag kept lunging at Wayne Flint, tongue hanging out, ready to wipe Flint's face with kisses. The other two fellows stood by, openmouthed but silent.

"Why don't we all go in for some root beer?" suggested Conte's mother. Her tone was bright, but she was wringing her hands.

Flint shook himself, got to his feet and said, "Man, I musta been totaled. Whew! What a trip."

"Wouldn't you like some root beer?" asked Conte's mom.

"Dear," said his dad, "I don't think the kids want any root beer. Let's you and I go have some."

Left alone with those three, Conte purposely avoided their eyes. All of them towered above him. All looked menacing. There was an extended silence. With a flick of his wrist, but without a word, Flint dismissed the other two. Obediently they went to the car.

"How'd you train your dog like that?" Flint asked, with an unmistakable note of admiration in his voice.

"Oh, you know," Conte said nonchalantly.

"Charlotta sent us," said Flint. "I didn't think I was gonna do anything. Charlotta's not my boss, you know," he said belligerently. "It's my own decision," he said. "Anybody with a dog like that can't be a total washout. What did you have in mind?"

Conte, speaking in monosyllables, opening his mouth

just a crack, explained the service he needed. "It's only temporary," he said, "until I can work out something else. You got someone who can do it?"

"A cinch," said Flint. "We'll use that little guy, Harry Mariot. I'll send him to your algebra class two or three times a week. All he has to do is wear your ski cap, right?"

"Right. Does he know any algebra?"

"Does he ever!"

"OK," said Conte. He was trying to decide whether or not to shake hands. What did gangsters do? In that moment Dag set up an excited barking from inside the house.

"I gotta split!" yelped Flint, and in a moment he had jumped into the car and was gone.

Conte's mother, sitting at the table drinking root beer, asked, "Why didn't you invite them in?"

Conte shrugged.

"To tell you the truth," she said, "that kid with the orange eyes gives me the willies. And why do they all talk out of the side of their mouth like that?"

"It's a local sickness," snapped Conte. "Comes from drinking too much root beer."

8 Flint the Fence Takes Over

It happens every October, along about the middle of the month. Call it the "squirrel-nut-gathering," the "bear-building-lair," the "get-off-your-lazy-butt" syndrome.

Crisp October, with its threat of winter, brings a certain frenzy. People as well as animals become possessed with a frantic urge to *do*. Little girls fix up their doll houses. Their mamas form new clubs. Small boys dump out their toy chests all over the floor to sort out their possessions and their lives. Older kids plow through their closets. And teachers are the worst of all. They start assigning homework as if there were no tomorrow.

October, they mutter, A month of school is already gone. Soon comes Thanksgiving, then Christmas, and we've done nothing but review! They panic. So they start to pile on the work. Book reports, term papers, charts, notebooks, tests, essays . . . it's always the same. Come mid-October, the teachers go bananas.

Conte kept his cool. Somehow he'd manage. He made certain changes in his lifestyle, each insignificant, perhaps, but combined they saved him many minutes a day.

He changed from button down shirts to slip-on T-shirts. (To button a shirt, would you believe it, takes twenty-seven seconds; slipping one over your head takes only five.)

Jeans and shirts were laid in piles on top of his bureau, easy to grab. To prevent the daily sock mix-up, socks were reduced to those all the same color—white—and never bundled together. When his tennis shoes wore out, Conte bought a pair of loafers, saving an average of sixty-four seconds a day. (It takes sixteen seconds to tie one lace.)

To his father's delight, Conte had his hair cut shorter than he'd worn it in the past two years. Combing time was cut in half.

Unfortunately, right smack in the middle of the already devastating October pile-on-the-work situation, the teachers got their latest issue of *Learn* magazine. The entire issue was devoted to the benefits of the "Project Method." So, they all went project-happy.

Mr. Stanley, the art teacher, decided that one art project, due in December, was not enough. Oh, no, the class had to submit an abstract pen and ink drawing and a "contemporary collage."

What did Conte know about abstract pen and ink

drawing? Nil. But he did know a thing or two about electric impulses and such. It took him about an hour, but in the end he had not only a suitable drawing, but a respectably scientific-looking model to present to Miss Worfenstein for HIC biology.

The invention was simple. Basically, when a metal stylus is attached to a power source, which in turn is wired to any audio-vibratory machine, the vibrations can be converted into symbols . . . in other words, as rock 'n' roll music boomed out of Conte's speakers, the stylus, dipped in India ink, made joyful leaps and squiggles upon a large sheet of white paper, creating an abstract drawing that was totally unique and, as Mr. Stanley later said, "Reminiscent of Turkish influence, yes, quite."

Miss Worfenstein was so ecstatic about the invention that she immediately began to pressure Conte about doing another project. The rewards of the faithful student, as Conte had always suspected, were simply that he got more and more and more work to do.

Miss Worfenstein would lie in wait for him outside the band room. "Oh, Conte, oo-whoo-whoo-whoo-whoo! You and I must discuss your next biology project." She held him there, with a hand on his sleeve, and, catching sight of Mr. Mott gave out another arpeggio giggle.

"Ohh! Mr. Mott! I came to tell you that I shall be

available to you on Tuesday afternoon."

Mr. Mott paled, then flushed, then stammered, "Uh—oh—um."

"Available to assist you with the band brochures," she continued.

"I—uh—well," said Mr. Mott, very red in the face, "I have planned to ask several students to come in and help, too. In fact, I've been meaning to ask Conte, here. Would you, Conte? I notice you spend a lot of time in the band room, and you seem very interested."

"I'd love to, Mr. Mott," said Conte. It was a beginning, and a good one, but where, oh, where would he get the time?

Mr. Morse, Conte's HIC history teacher, was pressuring Conte about undertaking some grand and noble project that could be displayed at the next Open House. Even sincere Miss Sommers was pushing for projects. "Transport yourselves," she coaxed, "into ancient times —why not create a replica of some fabulous shrine?"

Inwardly Conte groaned. He still had trouble enough just transporting himself into her class each day. She was beginning to get suspicious. Twice she believed his story, to explain his tardiness, "A bug flew in my eye." Then Conte miscalculated. He had forgotten that four times he had already used the same excuse, "My binder fell down and the rings broke open and all my papers fell out . . ."

"Why do you suppose you are having such bad luck with your notebook, Conte?" she asked. "Do you suppose that, psychologically speaking, you *want* to lose your papers?"

"Well, the truth is, Miss Sommers, I'm very clumsy."

"You are shaking, Conte. Are you sick?"

"Well, no—I guess it's from running, Miss Sommers."

"Why do you run so much, then?"

"Oh, I like to run, I guess. I really like it."

"Perhaps you should join the track team and do your running after school. I know Coach Brown is looking for people for the track team."

"Well, maybe I'll do that someday, Miss Sommers."

Yeah, someday, when he found what they were all after—Superproject. Even Mr. Gireaux was badgering him for a project.

They met once a week in the parking lot, right after fourth period. Mr. Gireaux, wearing his purple helmet, would already be astride his motorbike.

"Shakespeare!" he would shout above the roar of the engine. "If more people read Shakespeare!" *Vroom, vroom* went the motor. "They'd understand the old values, be satisfied with a slower, easier existence."

"How about Tom Sawyer?" Conte offered. He had read that back in fifth grade. It was really a classic—he'd already used it for four different book reports through the years.

"Why don't you do a project?" Mr. Gireaux adjusted his visor. "Do something from out of a Shakespearean play. One of last year's students—a girl—made a complete, authentic replica of the town where Shakespeare was born."

Conte groaned. There were some like that in every school—worse still, in every class. No matter what a guy did, somebody did something fancier, bolder, better. It would hardly surprise him if someday a student reconstructed the Battle of Gettysburg, bullets, bodies, and all, and got an *A* for it.

Pressure came, subtly, from Conte's parents. Lately they stared at him and sighed a great deal, then consulted each other in anxious whispers. His dad would say all too casually, "Something bothering you, son? Are you getting enough rest?"

His mother kept shoving vitamin pills at him and saying reassuring things like, "*We* love you, Conte," and "Grades are not all that important, Conte." And, thinking his troubles lay in a different area, she began to initiate little talks that came under the heading of Sex Education.

Conte shrugged them off. He knew perfectly well what they were thinking. They were thinking, "That kid's a nervous wreck. What'll we do? We'd better just assure him that we love him. We'll try not to pressure him."

But Conte's parents, by not pressuring him, somehow made him feel all the more pressured. Sometimes he wished his parents weren't so understanding. It made him feel as if he were living in a glass bowl.

Having met Wayne Flint, Conte was forever running into him. It was almost as if Flint were standing guard at Miss Merriman's door. It made Conte uneasy.

"Maybe he's just waiting for a friend," Greg suggested. "Or checking up on Harry Mariot."

"No," said Conte. "I think he suspects something. A guy like him—if he found out what I was doing—he'd even use blackmail, wouldn't he?"

Gloomily Greg nodded. "He's up to something, all right."

"Where'd he ever find that squirt, Mariot? The kid's only about four feet tall."

"Mariot's only twelve," Greg explained. "They let him come over from the grammar school to take math classes here. It's some new program. I think Flint's supposed to tutor him or something."

"Are you kidding? Flint?"

"He's a mathematical genius." Greg shook his head meaningfully. "I heard he got the highest math rating in the history of the school—over nine hundred points."

"And you think he goes to talk to Miss Merriman about math? I dunno. There's something funny going on. The other day he was standing out in the hall with a tape recorder."

Another day, Flint stood outside the door when Conte emerged from his fifth period algebra class. Firmly Flint planted himself in Conte's way. His mouth opened a mere slit.

"You're in two algebra classes," he said.

"There a law against it?" Conte challenged, looking tough, snarling.

"I won't say anything," Flint assured him. "It's OK with me if you want to take double algebra because some chick's in each of the classes, or whatever you've got in mind. I—are you particularly *attached* to Miss Merriman?"

"What are you talking about?" Conte cried. "*Merriman?*"

"Well, I just—I don't bother you and you don't bother me, right?"

"Right. Um—I heard you know a lot about math. I want to take the qualifying exam to get into geometry next semester."

"So? You're not going to learn any more by taking two periods of the same math."

"I know that. But—I heard sometimes you tutor people . . ."

"Ha!" It was a high-pitched squeal. "Forget it." Flint ducked into the classroom, and as he turned, Conte noticed that under his arm was a large book entitled *Adventures in Spain.*

Conte remained in the hall a moment longer and—yes, he actually did hear it. A low, soft, crooning laugh was coming from that room, from that teacher, that hag who each day was known to shriek out in ear-splitting decibels, "PAY ATTENTION!" This same Miss Merriman was laughing and cooing like a girl. She was putty in the hands of Wayne Flint.

The next morning, before second period algebra, there he was again, talking to Miss Merriman in the hall. In Flint's hand were several flashy brochures. Conte, glancing at one of them, saw the words, "Sunny Spain, Pleasant Portugal."

There was one problem. Conte didn't have enough time to see Pamela. He'd had high hopes for those Saturdays when the band marched in parades. Often they traveled long distances to march in competition against other high schools. They took off on the bus at seven in the morning, packed in with their instruments, all dressed in their splendid uniforms of purple and green.

Such plans as Conte had made for those Saturday outings! He and Pamela would sit together on the bus, laugh and whisper and walk together during the lunch break, sit in the bleachers together watching the performances of the other bands. . . . They would eat hot dogs together, drink a thousand strawberry sodas if that was what Pamela wanted . . .

But a marching band competition is a serious affair. It lasts the whole day long, and participants who have not been getting enough sleep during the week, tend to collapse sometime around noon.

Each band does its routine and is judged according to musical performance, marching style, and general appearance. General appearance meant grooming, and grooming meant Mrs. Dowdie. Mrs. Dowdie attended every event of the marching band, armed with scissors, razor, pancake makeup, and a tube of white acrylic paint. Her tools were applied, respectively, to unruly hair, fuzzy chins, pimples, and scuffed shoes.

In her own way, Mrs. Dowdie was an artist, as dedicated to her mission in life as any. She bullied and scolded, coaxed and cried. She whipped them into shape before each competition, and did it not for money—not for personal gain at all, do you hear?—but for the glory of Vista Mar High.

Woe to the boy or girl who backtalked Mrs. Dowdie; but bless you, dear, to the one who was the most cooperative. He or she was chosen for the singular honor of becoming First Lieutenant to Mrs. Dowdie. Who was chosen? Who? Conte Mark.

Yes, his was the honor of squirting out foaming lather, which Mrs. Dowdie roughly applied to somebody's stubble. It was he who bent down to daub somebody's smelly oxfords with paint, to hand out bobby pins and tie up ponytails to be tucked into tall beaver hats, both boys and girls alike, so that in the end they all looked like identical members of a clone, and but for differences in body type would have been indistinguishable.

Thus Conte Mark, rewarded for being cooperative, was deprived of the one thing he most desired—time, time alone with Pamela. If he happened to see her between classes, as he frequently did between first and second period, their moments together were slightly less than romantic.

"Why do we have to hurry so?" Pamela would be puffing, jogging behind him.

"Good exercise." Conte slowed down a bit.

"You know that midget, Harry Mariot?" Pamela began.

"He's not a midget. He's only twelve."

"Where'd he come from?" Pamela asked. "Why does he wear your hat? How come he's only in our algebra class when you aren't? Where do you go, Conte?"

Conte began to jog faster, hoping the movement would clear his thoughts. "Harry's sort of—well, he's the kind of guy that comes around when you need him. You know, like a genie who comes when you rub a lamp."

"You mean to tell me you rub a lamp and out comes Harry Mariot? You think I'm nuts?"

"Pamela, if a person is engaged in some vital business, about which another person is uninformed, that does not mean that the person doesn't trust the other person, but only that he would like to trust the other person if that other person would not be inconvenienced by it. Do you understand?"

"Sure," said Pamela. "But where do you go during second period?"

"I'm usually in the band room," said Conte, "working for Mr. Mott. We're planning the Christmas program," he said briskly. "We're deciding what songs to play, designing the programs, oh, lots of things. Mr. Mott needs me."

"But then why does Harry Mariot wear your ski cap?"

"His head's cold."

"It's been eighty-seven degrees!"

"You should see the kid in winter. Wears a parka when it gets down to sixty. Listen Pamela," he said softly, "let's go down to Katz."

"What? Now? We've got algebra . . ."

"Let's go down to Katz. I want to take my message off the tree."

"What about algebra?"

Conte only looked at her. In his heart there was a

yearning, a sudden and terrible yearning. And Pamela must have known it, for softly she sighed and softly she said, "All right, Conte."

And they went. They walked along the shore, and they told each other secrets—trivial things, but also monumental things, for everything is both trivial and monumental when two people feel this way about each other.

He had certainly never suspected that in a school the size of Vista Mar, an ordinary little thing would cause a big fuss. After all, no one had even noticed when he and Pamela had been gone a whole morning. This thing, this disaster, started quite casually in first period swimming the next day, when Coach Brown came out, blew his whistle and shouted for them all to line up and count out. It was the usual procedure. With eighty boys in the swimming class, they comprised four "teams" of twenty boys each.

For weeks they had been systematically swimming laps, team by team. "Three laps, breast stroke, team one!" *Tweet* went the whistle. The boys jumped in and swam, climbed out, *tweet* went the whistle, "Team two!" and so on.

But on this morning Coach Brown blew the whistle and shouted, "Team by team, jump in, float seven minutes."

Seven minutes! Float? Conte moaned and doubled over.

"Team one . . ." Coach Brown shouted.

Nineteen boys lined up at the edge of the pool, waiting for the "tweet." One boy stood shivering beside the teacher, saying, "C-Coach Brown, I c-c-can't . . ."

"Tweet," came the whistle. Nineteen boys immediately jumped into the pool. Nineteen boys submerged, floated to the top, arched their backs and lay upon the water.

"Coach Brown, I just can't . . ."

One boy was given a firm but gentle push by Coach Brown. Down he went, down into the green, then up, up, up. He arched his back, stretched out his arms and legs, even tried to take a breath . . .

Then he sank.

Conte sank down under the water, down like a stone. He came up once more, gasping and gagging, then down, down again nearly to the bottom where everything was green and weirdly wavery, and his own toes looked like wriggling white snakes.

The next thing Conte knew he was lying on a slab and thought to himself that he was dead and laid out in the morgue. He muttered to himself with surprise, "So this is how it feels to die! You hear echoes, but you can't see anything except red behind your eyelids—oh, where is my mother?"

He began to cry, great salty gurgling tears. He coughed violently. He felt himself being gently slapped on the cheeks. He opened his eyes to see Coach Brown's large black whistle nearly hanging into his face. He said politely, "Thank you, but I don't eat whistles." Then he heard someone saying, "The kid's flipped out."

The consequences of that particular episode were several and far reaching. Someone in the office was told to call the nearly drowned boy's mother, and they did. They telephoned his home and called "Mrs. Conte." The girl who happened to be working in the attendance office was Charlotta Jones.

Pamela, discovering Conte being carried off, failed to conceal her concern and gave way to real honest-to-goodness tears—so she became known as Conte's girl.

And Conte became known in a new way, too. In the eyes of Coach Brown he would always and forever be designated as "The Non-Floater." Thereafter, all directions to the class were given in duplicate. The coach would stand at the edge of the pool, blow his whistle and shout, "Teams, dive in, float two minutes, take five laps Australian crawl. Non-floater, dive in, take five laps Australian crawl, then *get out of the pool*!"

If the truth be told, that near-drowning episode had left Coach Brown terribly shaken. He vowed to be more vigilant. In particular, he made sure to keep his eye on that non-floater, that Mark what's-his-name, and he began to notice something funny about that kid. Every day, before P.E., after P.E., and sometimes between other classes and even at lunchtime that kid was running. Running to beat the band, by golly.

On Miss Merriman's desk lay several colorful brochures. They pictured azure water, cobbled streets, ancient church towers, and handsome matadors. For the past few days Miss Merriman had simply announced that the students might use their class time to do their assigned homework. She herself sat at her desk. She alternately gazed out the window and glanced at the travel folders. She smiled to herself, then sighed. When the bell rang, she seemed quite startled and screamed out unwittingly *"Pay attention!"* Then one day—it was a Thursday in mid-November—Miss Merriman was gone.

In her place was a substitute. Tan and heavily lip-sticked, the substitute was no great beauty, but quite an improvement over Miss Merriman. Her hair was flaw-lessly curled, frosted in color and nearly shoulder length. She sat at the desk, long legs outstretched, smiling.

Calmly the substitute smiled as the students came roaring in. Sweetly she smiled while the students yelled to each other across the room. Demurely she smiled as the class hour progressed and high spirits gave way to pandemonium. And when at last the bell rang, still she only gazed at the departing students and smiled.

It was then that Conte, gingerly approaching the substitute, realized that someone had achieved the ultimate in practical jokes. The substitute was a dummy.

9 CCC to the Rescue

Whoever did it was a genius, and Conte was filled with admiration. He was also distressed. Somebody else was working on a similar wavelength as he. Who? Who?

In a flash he knew precisely who.

When he told Greg about the stunt, his neighbor's eyes bulged in disbelief. Then Greg leaped up and began to pace furiously. He smacked his hand against his open palm, muttering, "How'd they manage it? How'd they get that dummy into the school?"

From the far corner of the dining room, where a huge tankful of yellow fishes played, Mrs. Gaff called out, "Lots of them are, you know. All over the place. Especially in education. You can't get rid of them, you know. Not if they have tenure."

She came into view in the living room, blinked her eyes several times at Conte. "Some people," she said, "have not the disposition to teach school. They ought not to be allowed. It is all a matter of—you know, one's inhibitions."

What in the world was she talking about? He could tell that even Greg was confused. Greg motioned for Conte to come down into his room.

"My mother," he said, "is a scientist, you know. She's very brilliant. Keen mind. Sharp intellect. In other words, she's got the smarts."

"I know," Conte said sympathetically. He had spoken to his dad about Mrs. Gaff. "She seems so preoccupied all the time."

His dad had said, nodding, "You like to observe people, don't you? You might make a good psychologist." Then he had said that maybe Mrs. Gaff sounded incoherent because her mind was always racing ahead to the next thing.

"That must be it," Conte said. "She ignores Greg, you know."

"Does she?" His dad had put down his newspaper. "Maybe she thinks it's the other way around."

Conte had thought about that. Maybe it did seem to Mrs. Gaff that Greg didn't care about her. Greg made no secret of his dislike for her fishes. Maybe Mrs. Gaff just quit trying to make herself understood because nobody listened anyway.

Of course, Conte said none of this to Greg. Greg was not the kind of person who would take advice. It was all so odd. Why couldn't people be normal? Why couldn't they be more like *him*?

Greg was shaking his head, muttering, "It had to be an inside job. I tell you, it's a brilliant caper. What I want to know is, who's getting the dough? The loot? The teacher's salary? It must add up to over a hundred bucks a week. How do they get the money?"

"The money," said Conte. "I hadn't thought of that."

"What a mind he's got, the guy who planned that caper!"

"What makes you so sure it was a guy and not a girl?"

"Dames don't think that way. They can't follow through. They fizzle out, go off on a tangent, get confused. No dame could carry off a thing like this."

"I think one did," said Conte.

"Naw."

"Bet you the $2.10 I owe you. Double or nothing."

"You're on," said Greg, thrusting out his hand. "And who do you think the girl is?"

"Charlotta Jones," said Conte, "without a doubt."

Charlotta, with her long taffy-blond hair hanging down so smoothly, so innocently, was not to be underestimated. Not by Conte, anyhow. She was smart. The fact that she never did any schoolwork proved it.

"Don't you ever go to class?" Conte asked her the next day. It was lunchtime. Most of the kids ate in the cafeteria, which was a madhouse. Conte, Charlotta, and a few other band members usually ate in the band room, happily sitting on the stools amid the dust and debris.

This time, since the cafeteria was featuring pizza, Conte and Charlotta were alone. Charlotta sat at Mr. Mott's desk, carefully peeling an apple.

"I don't go to class," replied Charlotta. "Not if I can avoid it. Oh, I usually check in at the beginning of the semester and once a week or so. The truth is, Conte," she said, giving his name a distinct emphasis, "nobody benefits when I go to class. Who needs me in class? The teachers don't. I certainly don't need to be there. And Mr. Mott needs me in the band room. Where could he find a secretary and caretaker and runner of errands, bringer of coffee— all that — for less than four hundred bucks a month?"

Conte said, "I hadn't thought of it that way."

"Sure," said Charlotta, nodding, still carefully paring the apple. "Listen, I work in the attendance office, too, assisting Miss Finkley. What do you think it would cost them to hire an assistant? Also, I do errands for Mr. Granberg. He sends me out for things like stamps and to buy the newspaper. Did you know that he and the custodians have a pool every day?"

"A pool?"

"Sure, they bet on things like who's going to win the ball game. If there's no ball game, they bet on other things like the stock market or even like how many murders will be committed that day. So," she said with a sigh, "I go where I'm needed. Fortunately," she said, "their needs fit in with my desires. I'd rather mess around with office work and stuff like that than listen to some boring lecture. I'm getting plenty of good experience by what I'm doing."

"But what about your grades?" asked Conte.

"Who cares about grades? It's not the style, Conte, to worry about grades. You start worrying about your grades and the next thing you know, they send you to the school shrink. They say you're maladjusted. You should know. Your dad's a shrink, isn't he? Anyhow, I'm not planning to go to college."

"What if you change your mind?"

She shrugged, carefully lifted off the last bit of apple peel and began to fashion a treble clef sign with the long strip. "If I wanted to go to college," she said, "I guess I'd just get a music scholarship."

"How could you?" Conte cried. "You don't even play an instrument."

"Stranger things have happened," said Charlotta, smiling. Painstakingly she began to mount the apple peel onto a large piece of cardboard, using a Popsicle stick and glue. Conte watched her, engrossed.

Charlotta asked, "Have you ever looked in those college scholarship catalogues?"

"Lots of times."

"You can get scholarships for lots of odd things. If I decide to go to college, there's a scholarship I've had my eye on. You get four years, all tuition and living expenses *paid*, if you will organize and maintain a gamelan band and be available for performances . . ."

"What the heck is a gamelan? . . .

". . . once a month," she concluded. "A gamelan band is—don't you know? There, you see, you go to class, but your education has been sadly neglected. You really ought to know what a gamelan band is. It's an Indonesian band, consisting of certain instruments—now, don't tell me you've never heard of a galoubet, either, or a gam bang."

"Seems to me," said Conte, "I've heard of something similar."

"So," said Charlotta, "all I'd have to do is round up some Indonesian kids and start a gamelan band, but—" She grinned. "Who needs it?"

"It is a good idea," said Conte smoothly. "Almost as good," he added, "as getting that dummy substitute. You know, she looks very real. It's a fantastic stunt."

Charlotta blew lightly on her fingernails, as if she had just polished them. "Think so?" She smiled to herself. "I think it was pretty good, too. Of course, I didn't do it all alone. I had a partner."

"Of course," said Conte, nodding. "Wayne Flint."

"Fifty-fifty," said Charlotta. "We split the proceeds."

She faced Conte earnestly. "It isn't that I need the money."

"I know."

"It was," she said, "the challenge."

"I understand."

Now Charlotta, eager to relive the glory of it, told Conte everything.

It all started when Wayne Flint had to do a research paper for his English class. He decided to do a paper about motivation. Flint the Fence decided to find out what causes people to make decisions—what *motivates* them.

"The idea expanded," Charlotta said. "Soon Flint decided it would be interesting to actually influence another person to do something that maybe they had never dreamed of doing. That way, he thought, you could really figure out exactly how that person had been motivated. Get it?"

Conte nodded. Obviously, the farthest thing from Miss Merriman's mind was a trip to Spain. Particularly in the middle of the school term. She had obligations! She had classes to teach! Even if she was old enough to retire twenty years ago.

Flint had worked his gentle but effective persuasion on Miss Merriman. The teacher, smitten with romantic notions of the Mediterranean, had decided to leave. That, said Charlotta, was where she came in.

"Wayne's smart," said Charlotta. "In fact, he's a mathematical genius. But he didn't quite grasp all the possibilities of a stunt like this. It was clear to me," she said, looking very pleased, "that if we could control the hiring of a substitute, if we could, in fact, just *pretend* to hire a substitute, the profits could be enormous. Well, you can imagine, Wayne loved the idea. He's always looking for ways to make money."

Conte nodded. From here, it was easy to reconstruct the entire situation.

"You made it your business to be in the office when Miss Merriman phoned in that afternoon, right?"

"Right. She didn't lie, either, and say she was sick. She just said she'd been called away, very suddenly, for a very urgent journey—a matter of life or death."

"Hers," said Conte, grinning. "Of course, you let Miss Finkley take that call."

"Of course. Normally Miss Finkley herself phones a substitute for the following day, but a slight accident occurred. Poor Miss Finkley got half a pot of coffee spilled on her skirt and had to go wash it off, so I . . ."

"So you called the substitute for her. Great! But didn't she tell you which person to call?"

"Oh, no. We just use a list that we have in the office. All I had to do was to add a fake name to the bottom of the list. Valerie Valasquez. How do you like that?"

"It's a good name. So, when Miss Finkley came back,

you told her you'd already phoned a substitute and you showed her the list, and maybe you even made a little joke about starting at the bottom of the list for a change."

"Exactly," murmured Charlotta.

"And in the morning," continued Conte, "you went to help out in the office again, and so you signed in for Valerie Valasquez and that was that."

"Later that day," said Charlotta, laughing, "Mr. Granberg went down the hall to see how things were going. He came back and told Miss Finkley how attractive the new substitute was. I thought I'd die, trying so hard not to laugh. She is attractive, don't you think?"

"Lovely," said Conte. "Where'd you get her?"

"That's where Wayne came in. I don't know where he found her. But he's got—you know—connections."

"But what about the money?" Conte asked. "How will you cash checks made out to Valerie Valasquez?"

"Simple," said Charlotta. "A couple of weeks ago I went to a bank in Arlington Hills and opened an account under the name of Valerie Valasquez. I won't go into the boring details of opening an account under an assumed name," she said with a toss of her head. "Suffice it to say, it can be done, and quite easily."

He had to hand it to Charlotta. She thought of everything.

Conte asked, "How do you keep the other students from telling?"

"What?" Charlotta seemed truly shocked. "What do you mean? Why would they care? Listen, a couple of them went into the office today to say what a great teacher Miss Valasquez is. They think it's a blast. Why would they care?"

"Because," said Conte, "they won't be learning any algebra. They won't be able to pass their college entrance exams. Take me, for instance. I was planning to take the qualifying exam after the first semester, so I could get into geometry . . ."

"Hmm," said Charlotta, biting her lip.

"Of course, I can probably study a lot of it on my own," Conte said. "But it seems to me I'll have to put up with the inconvenience and the worry, all because you and Wayne want to pull a stunt like this, and get rich while you're doing it. . . ."

Slowly Charlotta pulled herself up off the stool. Slowly she began to walk toward Conte, her arms outstretched. For it is the rare person among reformed sinners who doesn't backslide when the going gets rough.

"Maybe," Charlotta said, smiling suggestively, "somebody could make it up to you. For the inconvenience."

Something was pounding in his head, and Conte felt as if he were standing right inside the big kettle drum. He felt as he had never felt before, but also, to tell the truth, he felt scared.

Charlotta moved closer. Gently she pressed her body against his and whispered his name . . .

The door to the band room flew open. Conte heard voices. He saw people. One of them was Pamela Patterson, having come to get her flute.

That night Conte telephoned Pamela. Among other things he said, "Pamela, just because a person sees another person appearing to be doing something with a third person, don't you think that person ought to give the other person the benefit of the doubt, instead of assuming that the other person and the third person were doing something that would upset the person?"

Pamela said, "No." Then she hung up.

Perhaps the stars come into evil conjunction. Who knows exactly what causes it? Suddenly a dozen aggravations arise. One can be courageous in calamity. Or strong in adversity. But what do you do when everybody just starts *bugging* you at once?

Mr. Stanley the art teacher had the bright idea that from now on all the students would assemble on the lawn to become inspired and paint from Nature. That created a bit of a problem where band rehearsals were concerned.

At the same time, Mr. Mott was getting slightly hysterical when people failed to show up for rehearsals since the band was preparing for the Christmas concert and for the Thanksgiving game.

Miss Sommers, the sweet history teacher, was getting downright sticky. She was *demanding* that each student do a special project on ancient history.

Mr. Morse, Conte's HIC history teacher, expected Conte to come up with a project that was, in his words, "exotic and yet universally interesting."

Miss Worfenstein assailed Conte with her laugh. "Conte, yoo-hoo, oo-whoo-whoo-whoo-whoo! You must begin your next biology project. Soon, Conte, soon."

The dummy was still substituting, and Conte had to prepare for the qualifying exams in January, and there was nobody to help him.

His Mom was bugging him about taking his vitamins. His Dad kept muttering about keeping flexible. Greg was repeating double, triple, and quadruple, and Conte felt he was going out of his cotton pickin' mind.

It was the next to the last straw: Conte, running from HIC history to regular English, saw Coach Brown walking with Miss Sommers. Uh-oh. Each knew him by a different name. He sprinted past. Maybe they wouldn't notice him. But Coach Brown shouted out in surprise, "Why it's the non-floater, and he's running like sixty! I need him for the track team!"

The very last straw came when, home at last, Conte

found a nasty, sarcastic letter from the Comminger
Catalogue Company. It said:

> Dear Acct. No. a6401btx:
>
> It has been brought to our attention that you have
> suffered a lapse of memory. Your account is thirty
> days past due. Enclosed you will find a two-inch
> length of string. Tie it around your finger, dear Acct.
> No: a6401btx, so you will remember to send your
> remittance today.
>
> If we do not receive payment within fourteen days,
> we shall be forced to take legal action.

Along with the letter and the string, CCC had en-
closed its latest catalogue. This always mystified Conte
If they were so angry about his overdue bills, why did
they continue to send him catalogues?

Leisurely he began to browse through the catalogue.
Previous experience had taught him that if he ordered
something new, the billing department would leave him
alone for another month or so. Apparently the computers of CCC, busy processing his new order, would
forget about his overdue bills.

Conte laid down on the living room rug, absorbed in
the dazzling offers of CCC. He had been a subscriber
for seven years. Way back then his relationship with
CCC had already been one of hostility. At seven, Conte

had ordered a Put It Together Tick-Tock plastic clock for $19.89. With a weekly allowance of thirty-five cents, he had never fully recovered from this financial blow. And what Conte hadn't realized, at the ripe old age of seven, was that if he didn't pay his bills, CCC would charge interest. After nearly a year of angry correspondence from CCC, Conte's mother paid the original $19.89. To this date, the interest remained, and was regularly compounded.

Now Conte studied the array of items in the catalogue—mostly mechanical gadgets. His fascination with anything that worked automatically and/or could be dissected into a minimum of thirty pieces was like an inborn mania.

When he was just a baby, his parents had given him a playpen filled with toys. At the age of eleven months, Conte, using only an old teaspoon, had deftly removed every screw and bolt from the playpen, until the sides fell away and only the floor remained.

At fourteen months he took apart the musical teddy bear and rearranged its contents. Before he was three he had operated on the vacuum cleaner with a kitchen knife, and by the time he was six, Conte was into clocks. Literally *into*. They owned a large, walk-in grandfather clock that Conte had calmly disemboweled one afternoon and reassembled that night.

His parents begged him not to tinker with their clocks or to rewire the lights or to attach strange musical devices to the telephone. Conte tried hard to oblige. But at times he was seized with an overwhelming urge, and then he simply had to do it.

Now Conte pored over the catalogue, envisioning himself as an inventor of such marvelous gadgets as were displayed by CCC. There was a mechanical shoelace tier, a long handled device for people with stiff backs or protruding stomachs.

There was a flower pot that dispensed its own fertilizer and set off a little bell when it needed water. Oh, there were marvelous gadgets to solve every possible problem of man or beast. And sure enough, as Conte reached the last page of the catalogue, there was a device that would solve all his problems, too.

It had all the requirements. It was exotic, historic, modern, and scientific. It was attractive, portable, clean, and available in four sizes. Conte decided to order a large one. On his order form he printed the words PLEASE RUSH. Two weeks later, when he returned from school, Conte's mother met him at the door, looking alarmed.

"Conte, Conte, something has arrived for you," she said. "It's too big to bring into the house, so the man left it in the garage. The box has hieroglyphics and, oh, Conte, I'm afraid to ask you. Is it—could it be—Conte, did you order a mummy?"

"No," said Conte. "Don't worry. It's just an Egyptian pyramid."

10 Little Drops ...
Little Grains

Pamela's anger stemmed from two sources. First, she was convinced that Conte's truancy from second period algebra was proof that he and Charlotta Jones were having secret meetings. Secondly, Pamela felt strongly that a class ought to have a teacher.

"Maybe it's old-fashioned of me, Conte," she said heatedly, "but things have gone far enough. I'm going to the office to demand a real teacher."

"Pamela, honey—please," said Conte. "Don't do anything rash."

"Rash!" she shrieked. "Listen, I've got a dummy for algebra, and I'm tired of being told it's OK. It's not OK. She doesn't even *talk*."

Conte complained to Charlotta. The next day Harry Mariot appeared with something bulging under his jacket. At appropriate intervals during the period, from inside Harry's jacket came the unmistakable voice of

Miss Merriman screaming, "Pay attention!" Then it continued, elaborating about some theorem, but still Pamela was not satisfied.

Occasionally Flint the Fence wandered into the classroom to make minor adjustments on Valerie Valasquez. He repositioned her from time to time, or shifted the books around on her desk. Nobody knew exactly how and when Flint managed it, but the dummy possessed three or four different outfits and a variety of accessories, and wore them in turn.

It was all Conte could do to restrain Pamela from having a confrontation with Flint. She threatened to tell on him, to blackmail him, to write anonymous letters to the principal and the school board. "I've got to learn algebra!" she exclaimed. "I don't know how you're involved, Mark Conte, Conte Mark, but you can't make a fool out of me anymore. Listen, I've got to learn math or I'll never get off the ground—all my life I've wanted to fly, and all my life I've been told that I'll never . . ."

"You want to be a stewardess?"

Scornfully, disgustedly, Pamela shook her head. "I want to be a pilot," she said. "How can anybody be a pilot without knowing math?"

"How can anybody be a pilot," Conte asked, "if they don't know their right hand from their left?"

Wham! Pamela's foot shot out, and Conte felt a sharp blow to his shin. Instantly he grabbed her and shook her, hard, until Pamela was crying; and then he was holding her very tightly and saying, "Don't cry, Pamela, honey. I'll get you a teacher, I will."

Back to Charlotta, who wanted to know, "What's in it for me?"

Conte could only reply, "You name it."

"There's nothing I want," said Charlotta.

"Yes there is."

"What, Conte?"

"Power."

"Huh—power? What power?"

"I'll get you some."

"How?"

"Trust me, Charlotta. You and I understand each other. You—you're the type that needs a challenge, or you're bored to death. Am I right? Of course I'm right. Listen, I'm gonna get you a challenge like you never had before, and I'm gonna get it for you soon, very soon. Now, you get Wayne Flint into that classroom. Can you do it?"

Coolly, Charlotta nodded.

Whatever her method, Conte didn't need to know. It was enough that the very next day when the second period algebra class was assembled, they were met by a firm, authoritative voice.

"All right, you guys, sit down and shut up, and open your books to page fifty-two. Anybody doesn't like it

can get out right now and lose credit for the whole semester. Now you cats listen and listen good, 'cause I'm
only going to explain this concept once, and you're
gonna be tested on it tomorrow. . . ."

Pencil points no longer broke. People did not need
drinks of water. Tardiness was a problem of the past.

As for Flint the Fence, a strange change came over
him. Kids who had known him for years were astounded. Wayne Flint was actually happy. Not only
did he teach during class time, but he tutored those who
needed extra help after school. With freshman compre-
hensive tests coming up, Flint was taking no chances on
his students making a bad showing.

Mr. Stanley, the art teacher, considered himself as something of a philosopher. Not content only to teach color,
design, and technique, he regularly mimeographed papers on which were written "Lessons for Life" or
"Thoughts for Today."

Most often, Mr. Stanley's sayings had nothing whatsoever to do with art. At times they were even unin-
telligible. Once, for example, he mimeographed the
legend from a yogurt carton, FRUIT AT BOTTOM, and
spent several paragraphs trying to distill some profound
meaning from it.

Conte had been able to resolve the conflict between
his art class and the band. With Mr. Stanley wanting pa-

pers mimeographed, and Mr. Mott needing to have programs and brochures and instructions mimeographed for the coming Christmas concert, Conte took over that function for both teachers. Nearly every fourth period he spent in the "copy machine room." He usually worked very fast, or got some other student to assist him, so that he might at least make part of the class in either art or music. Naturally, for whichever class he missed, the teacher assumed he was busy with the mimeographing.

The situation was strained, but not drastic—until the approach of December 3, due date for art projects. Then Conte began to experience certain familiar symptoms. Hot flashes. Itching palms. Breaking out in a cold sweat. In other words—panic.

He confided in Greg. "The truth is," he said, "I'm not at all artistic. I've never been able to draw or paint."

"Why not use some of your mother's art?" Greg asked.

"What?" Conte exclaimed. "Steal my mother's work? Put my name on something another artist has done?" He sighed. "I already tried that. My mom caught me."

"What'd she say?"

"She said," Conte replied, "two very bad words."

"Gee," said Greg admiringly, "my mother would never say anything like that. She's so square, so old-fashioned, I mean, she just isn't *with it*."

"What will I do for an art project?"

Greg pursed his lips and frowned. He pulled at his chin as if a real beard grew there. "Multi-media, you say? That means it could be three-dimensional, right?" He pondered further. Then he jumped up and said brightly, "Say, do you want to use some of my mother's fishes? I mean, you could mount them onto a piece of plywood or something, and present them as a kind of collage."

"Forget it. They'd stink." Conte was silent for a moment. Then wonderingly he said, "Greg, you really do hate those fish, don't you?"

"I guess I do," said Greg soberly. "Sometimes I dream about them, how I'll go and stab them or electrocute them."

"Why do you feel that way about the fishes?"

"I hate fish!"

"Do you eat fish?"

"No! No!" Greg cried. "I do not eat fish. I couldn't. It would be like . . ."

"What?" Conte prompted.

Greg had begun to pace wildly. "How could I? Never. Never. It would be like eating my own . . . my own . . ." Abruptly he stopped pacing, faced Conte and said, "Would you believe it? I'm jealous of those fishes. I—I act as if they were my brothers and sisters!"

Conte, nodding, murmured encouragingly, "Do you?"

"Of course that's it!" Greg exclaimed. "Can't you see

it? I won't eat fish because in a way it would seem like cannibalism to eat a fish, because they've always been around. Ever since I was born, like people, for heaven's sake."

"Does your mother eat fish?" Conte asked.

"Sure she does! She loves it—shrimp and sole and lobster. Those fish are no relatives of mine!" he yelped. "My Mom is always bending over them and talking to them, but they're not people. They're just fish."

"True," said Conte. "Now, can we work on my art project?"

"What a dope I've been," Greg said, smacking his head with his hand. "What an idiot. Conte, you ought to consider becoming a shrink. I mean, you understand people. . . ."

"I might do that, Greg. Now, can we get to my art project?"

"Later! Later! There's something I have to do first. I'm going to go to the store and buy a lobster. I'll eat it for dinner." And he was upstairs in a flash calling out, "Mother! Mom! Mater, O Mother of mine."

She stood bent over the largest of the tanks, which was lighted by a blue bulb. As Greg came in shouting, Mrs. Gaff whirled around. Her face seemed to crumple and sorrowfully she said, "Oh, son, you have just interrupted the courtship dance of my yellow-headed jawfish from the Florida reefs."

"I'm really sorry," Greg said. He told his mother he

would need about seven dollars. To Conte's astonishment, Mrs. Gaff didn't even ask why. She merely said, "Go get it, then, from my purse."

Conte went with Greg to the store where they bought a lobster. Later, Conte watched while Greg ate it. "You know, Greg, you're really lucky," he said.

"How so?" Greg asked, still chewing.

"It isn't everybody who can get liberated in a few minutes, just by eating a lobster."

"What do you mean?"

"I mean, you're getting rid of your hang-up about fish by eating one, and you'll never feel jealous again, because now you know you've got power over fishes. Of course, you always did have power over them. Did you notice how fast your mother gave you that money? That's because she always gave you credit for brains."

Greg paused, his fork in the air. "What do you mean?"

"Well, look at it this way. Compared to a fish, you're a mental giant."

Greg nodded. "I see what you mean. Is that why she gives me everything I want?"

Conte nodded.

"I see. She always figured I was super-smart—compared to the fish—so if I asked for something, she figured it was necessary and important. She sees me as a rational being!"

Conte said, "What am I going to do for my art project? We've spent most of the afternoon fooling around with fish."

Greg picked up the lobster shell, still nearly intact, and said with a smile, "Here is your project."

"What?"

"I'll give you a big piece of plywood. You've got driftwood and scrub brush and sand. Use the lobster shell for part of the collage. It's raw nature. Can anybody improve on raw nature?"

Conte nodded. "I see what you mean. I'll have to think of a title."

"A title is the main thing," Greg agreed. "Especially where Mr. Stanley's concerned."

Conte went home with the plywood and the lobster shell. Outside in the yard he prepared his masterpiece, mounting the lobster shell smack in the middle of the plywood with glue. He added a single piece of driftwood on the right, some scrub brush on the left. It was very stark. That would make it very meaningful. Inside, Conte found a piece of shirt cardboard and printed the title: OUR ENDANGERED SEASCAPE.

Conte went to bed contented. Just because he didn't know what the MESSAGE was, didn't mean a message didn't exist, did it? No doubt Mr. Stanley would find one. Conte closed his eyes contentedly. It's all in the way you look at things, he told himself. One did not need to work one's tail off. One needed only to have the right perspective on things.

During the night Conte heard only a single yelp from Dag, followed by a long, low howl.

In the morning Conte went out to get OUR ENDAN-GERED SEASCAPE. He found that it had not only been endangered, but fully destroyed. The lobster shell was ripped off and chewed. The driftwood was no more than a pile of soggy splinters. The scrub brush had totally disappeared.

It was six-thirty. He had to get to fencing class. Soon Greg would begin to honk the car horn, urging him to hurry.

Time! Time! Time!

In back of his mind Conte remembered one of Mr. Stanley's little "thoughts for the day." It was a poem:

Little drops of water, little grains of sand
Make the mighty ocean, make the pleasant land . . .

He remembered, too, an artistic principle that the teacher had stressed. "Use a great many of something—or very few."

Conte had checked that point with his mother. She agreed. In a collage of postage stamps, for example, it would be interesting to use dozens of them. For a thing found in nature, like a leaf, it might be better to use a single one, thus highlighting its uniqueness.

Honk! It was Greg's horn.

Conte snatched up the plywood, brushing off the residue. He picked up a handful of sand and stuffed it into his pocket.

Honk! Honk! Laden with books and supplies, Conte rushed to the car where Greg waited, scowling.

"What's all that junk for?"

"My art project. Dag ate the lobster shell. This will be even better."

"What are you going to put on that board?"

"A grain of sand."

"*One* grain?"

"Yup."

"Conte, are you kidding? Have you flipped? Are you stoned?"

"Not at all," said Conte. "When you use just one of something that is usually found in profusion, it becomes very important. I'm going to call it, "Little Drops —Little Grains." First, though, I'm going to paint the whole board solid red. I'll do that during fencing period. Get Downer to answer roll call for me, wearing my mask."

"Conte—*one* grain?"

"Mr. Stanley will love it. You'll see."

Mr. Stanley had arranged to provide ribbons for the best works of art, hoping to inspire students to participate in the county-wide art show to be held in spring. He explained that he had based the awards on "design, aptness, originality, and universality."

The students gathered around the three winning art works. The first prize winner was a tremendously large hibiscus made of coffee cans and tissue paper, welded onto a piece of lead pipe. The second was an oil painting on canvas, picturing about three hundred thumbs combined with a dozen three-dimensional thumbs made of plaster. It was titled: THUMBS.

The third prize winner was Conte's masterpiece, LITTLE DROPS—LITTLE GRAINS.

"Notice," said Mr. Stanley, pointing delicately with his pointer, "this faint ripple effect . . ."

Conte felt his face getting hot. That was where the paint had dripped.

"See," said Mr. Stanley, still pointing, "how the entire composition depends upon the effective placement of the grain of sand. Had the grain been here—or here—well, you can see for yourselves that such a choice would have created *disharmony* rather than *balance*."

Conte's classmates stared silently at the painting.

Mr. Stanley said he had high hopes for his students, and he hoped that now all were stimulated and inspired.

Conte felt dazed. Man, oh, man! Success!

After class he ran pell-mell, heading from the art building to the band room. He felt that, like a person of

mythology, he ran on winged feet, faster and faster, flying . . .

"Non-floater!" a voice boomed out at him, and before Conte could escape, he felt Coach Brown's hand on
the back of his neck. Coach Brown said, "I want you to
report to the gym after school today, non-floater. We
need you for the track team."

"But . . ."

"Only three afternoons a week."

"I can't . . ."

"Mr. Morse tells me you're a student of his for HIC
history. Mr. Morse has agreed to give you some history credit for being on the track team."

"But how . . ."

"Don't worry; it'll all come out right in the end.
Someday you might be getting P.E. credits for taking
history. It's all the same. We educate the *whole* child
here, you see."

"But, Coach . . ."

"If you go out for track, you won't have to swim
anymore."

"But what about the Ace Laundry and Mr. Peeches
. . ."

"Are you feeling quite all right? Never mind—just
run. Keep running. That's a boy—run, run!"

11 Won't You Come into My Pyramid?

Some people say that pyramids possess a rare, a mystical, an almost magical power. Pyramid power. They say that mummies in the great pyramids of Egypt were preserved not because of any mumbo-jumbo or bandages soaked in special solution and wrapped tightly around. No—they say that preservation was caused by the *shape* of the pyramid itself. Thus was born the theory that states that a pyramid, by its very shape, exerts a certain power on the objects inside it.

The company that manufactured Conte's pyramid claimed that it had astonishing effects on people, animals, plants, and even objects. "Pyramid power" could sharpen dull blades, keep food from spoiling, increase fertility in plants, and as for humans—it would stimulate the intellect and enhance the sex drive.

Conte planned to test these claims scientifically. The investigation would give him biology credit. He'd get

English credit for writing a composition on his findings. An account of Egyptian pyramids and mummification would count as a history project. Somehow he'd try to make an art project of it too.

The very shape of a pyramid attracts the eye and excites the imagination. People see it variously as a place to work, to sleep, to create, to love.

When Conte brought the pyramid to school, Miss Worfenstein gazed at it longingly. Then softly she trilled her delight, all the way down the scale. She exerted all her influence and got permission from Mr. Granberg for Conte to set up his pyramid and conduct his experiments at Katz Beach.

Made of sturdy cardboard with a plastic coating, the pyramid was light, yet waterproof. Katz Beach was the perfect place for it, giving Conte easy access *and* privacy. It turned out to be just what Conte needed—a place to sit quietly and pull himself together.

Now that he was going out for track, Conte rarely got home before five. While jogging around the track, he tried to memorize facts and dates, but it was a strain to study while running, and a definite hazard to his health. Often he tripped and skinned his knee, or worse.

When he wasn't working out for Coach Brown, Conte spent afternoons helping Mr. Mott get things ready for the Christmas program and for Saturday performances of the marching band.

Fortunately, he had been ousted from his exalted post as First Lieutenant. Mrs. Dowdie said she needed someone more alert, someone who wouldn't shame her by falling flat on his face right in front of the reviewing stand. So Conte was able to concentrate on Pamela, planning wonderful diversions for the two of them. They often sat on the grass under a tree, where he read to her from his assigned material, *Hamlet,* or "Socio-Political Causes of Revolution." She really seemed very interested. It was Conte's head that would begin to bob, until he was fast asleep. When he awakened, Pamela would have gone off to eat lunch with Kurt Zelinkowitz, the rat.

With whom could he discuss such problems? He found that Mr. Mott was a willing listener, nodding encouragement, saying little. He told Mr. Mott about Comminger Catalogue Company with its wonderful wares. He talked about Coach Brown nabbing him for the track team, about taking fencing, and having won a ribbon for his art project, about wiring his telephone, and Mr. Mott nodded and said, "You've got a busy schedule, haven't you?"

He told him about Pamela going off with Zelinkowitz, and Mr. Mott seemed to understand.

"He's stealing my girl, that rat. I happen to know he took her to the show last Friday night. My neighbor saw them there."

"Hmm," Mr. Mott said, frowning.

"And I know they were making out. Why do girls go for guys like Zelinkowitz?"

"Hmm?" shrugged Mr. Mott.

"I'd like to take that Zelinkowitz and stuff the piccolo down his throat."

"Hmm!" exclaimed Mr. Mott.

"Mr. Mott, do you think I should call her tonight?"

Mr. Mott nodded, "Hmm."

"Yeah, I think I will. You know, you've got good ideas, Mr. Mott."

One day Mr. Mott looked squarely at Conte and said, "You know, Conte, it seems to me that you're going to have to re-order your priorities."

"Hmm?"

"I mean, Conte, you can't do everything, can you? Do you want to go out for track, or would you rather do fencing? Will you spend your after-school hours on music or art? What's more important to you, Pamela or spending all your extra time on your stereo?"

"Hmm!" exclaimed Conte. "My dad always tells me to be flexible."

"You are as flexible," said Mr. Mott, "as an octopus. Unfortunately, there is only one of you, and you are trying to do activities enough for three."

"Two," said Conte, but Mr. Mott seemed not to hear him.

"When Charlotta graduates next year," he said, "I'll

be needing an official student assistant. Charlotta has been well—rather unofficially my assistant these past years. She knows nothing about music but—you see, I know that being in the band has really helped her. She used to be—well, she was a little mixed-up and headed the wrong way last year; but now, I can honestly say that being in the band has helped her to—well, to redefine her goals. She's a nice girl."

"But . . ." said Conte.

"I realize that you were student conductor in intermediate school," Mr. Mott continued. "It would be something to work toward here. You have the ability and the drive. Think about it, Conte."

Suddenly Conte could think of nothing to say. There was a strange, cloudy, stinging sensation in his head, right behind his eyes. That night he sat up late in his room, furiously polishing his trophy with toothpaste and the little rag, thinking about Mr. Mott's offer.

Late—past midnight—Conte's mother tiptoed into his room and, finding him awake, sat down on the bed to talk.

"I hardly ever see you," she said. "You just eat your dinner and run upstairs to work."

"Yeah. Well, that's how it is in high school. Lots of homework."

"How did it go with your art project? You didn't even tell me."

Conte stopped polishing and looked up, grinning.

"Hey—I got third place. A ribbon. Mr. Stanley thought it was great."

"You didn't show it to me."

"I will. It's still at school."

"What's it like?"

"I—oh, I'll bring it home tomorrow. You'll see it then," Conte said. Then he added, "Mr. Mott said I could become student conductor. I'd have to put in some extra time. I'm not sure it's worth it."

"Oh, right," she said. "Especially since you hate band. All that extra work, and for what? A crummy trophy. Another cheap thing that just stands around getting tarnished." She sniffed, hard, and Conte got down under the covers to escape.

The next day, when Conte brought home his masterpiece painting, LITTLE DROPS—LITTLE GRAINS, his mother gazed at it for a long time. Then she stared at him. She cocked her head and said, "Are you putting me on?"

Conte shook his head soberly.

Without even a sniff and without a word, she stomped out of the room and into her "garret," and from it came such a pounding and clattering as Conte hadn't heard since the time she got mad at the "old biddies" who had tricked her into serving on a committee for the community bazaar.

Conte ran to her "garret," poked his head in the door, and shouted, over the pounding, "What's wrong? Why are you so mad?"

"Because you're a fraud!" she shouted back over the din.

"My teacher loved it!" Conte screamed back.

"Then he's a fool!"

"It makes a STATEMENT!"

"Then the statement is a lie!"

"How can you say that? It's modern art. It's original and ingenious. My teacher . . ."

His mom said a bad word about the teacher. His dad, just home from work, said it was poor psychology for mothers to say words like that about teachers. Speaking of poor psychology, Conte said, his mom had insulted his painting. Thereupon his dad, seeing the red plywood and the almost invisible grain of sand roared, "Son, that is absolutely the worst excuse for a work of art that I have ever seen in my life."

Thus, it was a good thing he had a haven—his pyramid, where he could get away from it all. He'd show them. They didn't appreciate his talents. What kind of parents talk to their child like that, insult his artwork? He couldn't wait to get out of the house—couldn't wait. Just another year and a half and he'd be in Chicago, maybe caught in a blizzard and freezing to death. That'd show them. Pamela would go around with that creep, Zelinkowitz. Maybe they'd even get married and have a bunch of kids, all amber-eyed. Talk about being a pilot

—ha! That dope didn't even know her right hand from her left, so how could she fly a plane?

Now that he didn't have to take swimming anymore, Conte could spend first period working on his pyramid experiments. Down at Katz Beach, safely tucked inside his pyramid, Conte was as happy as a clam in off-season.

He worked carefully and intently, keeping scientific records of his findings. While he worked he envisioned himself wearing a white lab coat and working (with seven assistants under him) in a multi-million dollar laboratory funded by the United States government, the U.N. and a giant corporation called Flint and Jones, Ltd. In his laboratory (he'd pronounce it lab*o*ratory, as the British do) he'd discover universal truths. He'd invent incredible machines. He'd propose stunning new theories.

The experiments actually taking place inside that pyramid were considerably less dramatic. From home Conte had brought a large cushion to sit on and a small table. Onto the table he put a bit of raw hamburger, a raw egg in a dish, a piece of Swiss cheese, some bread, and a small bowl of milk. Naturally, as dictated by proper scientific method, he used a "control." He set up identical items in Miss Worfenstein's office. He set up a second "control" in Mr. Dean's classroom, so that he could also get credit in his regular biology class.

Everybody involved with the pyramid study added suggestions of his own. Conte's dad suggested that he perform psychological studies. Mr. Dean wanted Conte to test pulse, heartbeat, and other bodily functions. Miss Worfenstein was most interested in the emotional effects of pyramid-sitting. She wanted Conte to devise ways of measuring joy, contentment, and love.

Although Conte kept his experiments pretty much to himself, word got around. People began to drop by on Conte in his pyramid. They began to ask for favors. "Hey, could I keep my soda pop in your pyramid?" One elderly gentleman said it helped his arthritis just to stand in the shadow of the pyramid. A lady brought her puppy who'd been suffering from fleas and swore the pyramid cured him. Some of the surfers dropped by and said that sitting in the pyramid helped them get their heads together.

Conte planned to spend most of his Christmas vacation in the pyramid, perhaps even to sleep in it all night. But Christmas vacation turned out to be a bummer.

Pamela and her parents went away to Arizona, and Conte contracted what the doctor called "a touch of viral pneumonia." How the doctor could call it "a touch" was beyond Conte. He felt worn out, done in, weak, tired, and miserable.

When Conte wasn't sleeping or eating chicken pies and oranges (the two foods his mother served whenever anybody was sick), he was talking on the telephone. Who was he talking to? Wayne Flint. What did they talk about? Algebra.

Thus, Conte was vigorously tutored in algebra throughout the entire vacation. He hated every minute of it.

12   The Amazing Reform of Flint

By the end of the semester, it became clear to the office that Miss Merriman wasn't likely to return. Miss Finkley telephoned Miss Merriman's home many times. Mr. Granberg, fearing the worst, drove to her apartment to find it locked up and abandoned. None of the other teachers had heard from Miss Merriman. At last it was discovered that Gladys Hutchinson, the woman who worked in the cafeteria, had received a postcard from Miss Merriman. The postmark was Algeria. It bore the puzzling message, "What they say about the Casbah is true, so true."

In the teachers' lounge and at teachers' meetings the question was debated: "Should Miss Merriman be fired?"

No, no, cried her defenders. Just because she wasn't present at the school didn't mean Miss Merriman should lose her job. In fact, maybe she had gone to Algeria to further her own experience and education. In that case, Miss Merriman ought to get a raise.

The opposition objected. Give a raise to a teacher who had left the country? Why, that was just as absurd as continuing to pay the salary of a teacher who had died.

Angrily the defenders pointed out that Miss Merriman was *not* dead. And anyhow, nothing in the entire education code said a teacher has to be alive in order to get paid!

After long and bitter debate, the school board decided to take decisive action. Specifically, they would hang loose, sit tight, do nothing. Miss Valasquez, the charming substitute, could stay on. She was doubly appreciated because she never caused any trouble at teachers' meetings, never bothered the office by asking for extra supplies, didn't antagonize the parents by complaining about their kids. She was, in fact, the perfect teacher.

In February, when the results of the freshman algebra placement test became known, Mr. Granberg was even more delighted. The test results were the highest in the history of Vista Mar High. Miss Valasquez had evidently given special, personal help to several of the students. They had been able to pass the entire year's work and were now eligible for an accelerated special course in geometry.

So pleased was Mr. Granberg with the teaching skills and dedication of Miss Valasquez, that he sent her a formal letter congratulating her and inviting her to give a speech at the very next teachers' meeting. He suggested her topic to be "Cultivating and Harvesting the Seeds of Learning." Thus would she inspire the other teachers.

So far Miss Valasquez had been conveniently ill whenever it came to attending teachers' meetings. Each time she missed a meeting, Miss Valasquez sent a proper and plausible note to Mr. Granberg. This time, however, the request for her presence was made several weeks in advance.

"I shall meet you in front of your classroom," Mr. Granberg had written formally, "to escort you personally to the meeting."

Well, the jig was up. There was nothing to do but to get Charlotta busy with pen and paper. Miss Valasquez sent an elaborate farewell letter and disappeared from Vista Mar High as suddenly as she had arrived, leaving behind her some excellent math scores and tender memories. For, once she was gone, the other teachers (proud of being a very close-knit group), began to speak of "our dear Valerie" with respect and affection.

The departure of Valerie Vasasquez left poor Wayne Flint with nothing to do. He became sullen and surly. Downer and Zelinkowitz tried in vain to cheer him by proposing all sorts of capers. Flint would only fold his arms and say disdainfully, "Kid stuff." Even Charlotta couldn't talk Wayne out of his depression.

Conte saw him sometimes, hanging around outside the algebra classroom, looking as pathetic as a lost pup. The new algebra teacher, a brisk gentleman who had formerly taught at a military academy, ignored Flint. Wayne had proposed to the teacher that he might need a student assistant. No dice. So Flint was lonely and depressed.

"I am," he told Conte frankly, "having an identity crisis."

"What?"

"I don't know who I am," said Flint. He glanced around the empty halls, then ducked his head and whispered, "What I really want to do is be a teacher."

"Then, why not?"

Flint frowned. "It's my reputation," he whispered.

"Don't worry about that," said Conte. "Anybody can make a mistake. I'm sure a lot worse guys than you have turned out to be schoolteachers."

"That's not what I mean," said Flint, looking pained. "I mean my reputation with the guys."

Conte nodded. Poor Flint looked so despondent that Conte offered the only solace he could. He said, "Would you like to go and sit in my pyramid?"

"What good's that going to do me?"

"I'm not sure, but strange things are happening to people in the pyramid."

"What things?"

"Oh, people say they feel different in the pyramid."

"How different?"

"Some feel good, more peaceful. Others feel excited. You know—charged up. Turned on. It's strange."

Flint decided it was worth a try. The following Saturday he went down to Katz Beach and sat in Conte's pyramid for a full four hours. When he finally emerged, witnesses swore it was a different Flint from the one who had entered. He seemed to be standing slightly taller, and there was about him an air of serenity. His features seemed to have softened, his movements mellowed.

Later it became legend. People recalled Flint's first words upon stepping from the pyramid. "I'm so ——— thirsty I feel as if I've been in a sauna bath for a week." Then he continued. "The ——— with everybody. I'm going to graduate from this place and go to university and become the best ——— teacher you ever saw!"

Teachers were to ponder for months the change that came over Wayne Flint, one of their "extremely bright but undermotivated youngsters." His record for malicious mischief, laziness, and crime went all the way back to his kindergarten years.

Volumes are written about such transformations.

Government grants are given so people can find out how such educational miracles happen.

Coach Brown attributed it to his physical fitness program.

The English teacher attributed it to a film the students had seen, titled, "The Relationship of the Lemur to the Evolution of Man." She wrote a glowing report to the film company. The film was later adopted statewide.

Wayne's counselor attributed the change to a new kind of therapy he'd been using with the boy. Namely, the "Cop-Out Technique." In this method the counselor answers every comment and question with the words, "Maybe yes. Maybe no. What do you think?" If this technique doesn't force the student to make his own decisions, at least it makes him stop pestering the counselor.

Most people attributed Wayne Flint's reform to the inspiration of one Valerie Valasquez. She was nominated as "Teacher of the Year."

It was a great blow to Charlotta Jones to have Flint going straight. What would she do with her time? Her energy?

"It isn't just the money," she told Conte.

"I understand," he said.

"You promised me power," she reminded him. "You said everything would be great if I got Wayne to teach algebra, and now . . ."

"Charlotta," said Conte, "have you ever thought of graduating early?"

"What for?"

"So you could be with Wayne, for one thing. If he goes off to college he might meet someone else."

"True," said Charlotta. "I've been thinking about that."

"You probably have enough units to graduate this June," Conte said. "You get extra credit for all this office work."

Charlotta nodded. "I went to summer school last summer, so I do have enough units. But I need a science course in order to graduate."

"That's what I'm getting at," said Conte. "You can take computer science."

"Is that science?" she asked doubtfully.

"Doesn't it say 'science'? I'm sure you can get your counselor to approve it. Mr. Kelly needs people like you in the computer class. You've got office skills. You've got experience."

Charlotta looked at him suspiciously. "What's in it for you? Why do you want me to take computer science?"

"Well, frankly," he said, "I want you to graduate early so I can be Mr. Mott's assistant next year. He even said I might become student conductor. I can't do it with you here. I can't compete with you, Charlotta."

She smiled slightly. "Really?"

"Really," he said.

"But, Conte, how do I get power by taking computer science?"

"Honestly, Charlotta—you must be kidding. Don't you know that this whole school is run by a computer? Every university, every giant corporation in the country —even the Pentagon—is run by computer. And you ask me about power . . ."

"But what are *you* going to do for me?" she persisted. In Charlotta's code of ethics, a promise had to be kept, no matter what.

"I will let you use my pyramid."

"Pooh! Everybody uses that pyramid. All they have to do is sign up for one of your experiments, and then they sit in the pyramid. Big deal."

"It is a big deal. From now on, they're going to have to pay for the privilege. You," said Conte, "will be the only person who gets to sit in the pyramid free."

Charlotta was satisfied. Conte could tell that large-scale schemes were already being hatched in her head for the day when she knew about computers.

It was true that Greg and Conte had decided that unless they charged an admission fee to the pyramid, Conte would soon run out of volunteers. People will line up to do almost anything if they have to pay for it.

The pyramid really did seem to exert a certain

unique power. People who had sat in it swore it heightened all their faculties.

Conte had begun modestly, duplicating experiments he had read about. When it came to testing food spoilage, the results were inconclusive. No matter what you do, raw egg, hamburger, cheese, bread, and milk get smelly, slimy, and repulsive after a few days—pyramid or not.

When it came to sharpening knives and razor blades, sometimes the pyramid did make a difference. After a week or so of lying in the pyramid, a blade seemed sharper than before. Still, on the other hand, sometimes the opposite was true.

The spectacular results of pyramid power occurred not with food or objects, but with living things—plants, animals, and people. A sweet potato placed inside the pyramid in a glass of water began to sprout most vigorously. Within five weeks it was a green, leafy, luscious plant. Conte took his mother's African violets, half-dead from neglect, placed them inside the pyramid for a week, and they prospered. The day after he'd first set up the pyramid, Conte had noticed two snails crawling in the sand. He put them into a five-quart cider jug, added several leaves, and placed the jug inside the pyramid. The next time he checked, the snail population was exploding right out of the jug.

Conte told Greg about it. Greg told his mother. And

the following Saturday morning, there stood Greg and Mrs. Gaff, carrying the tank with her unmated yellow-headed jawfish from the Florida reefs. Inside the pyramid, the yellow-headed jawfish did finally mate. Mrs. Gaff was ecstatic.

Somehow, after that morning, a beautiful bond developed between Greg and his mother. They *communicated*. Greg thought the pyramid had a lot to do with it.

Conte consulted his dad. Could it really be that the pyramid exerted a supernatural influence on people?

Conte's dad said he didn't know. "Figure it out for yourself," he said. "You've got a good head on your shoulders."

It annoyed Conte. He'd heard that same sentence a million times. If a person had to figure everything out for himself, what was the use of having parents? They told him to be independent. Fat chance. Whenever he tried to be independent—like the time he wanted to go hop a freight car to Canada—they said he was crazy.

The pyramid thing was getting out of hand. The more hours Conte spent on the project, the more he wanted to do. One idea gave birth to three or four more, until it seemed he could easily devote the rest of his life to studying pyramid power. Too bad he had to go to school. Oh, how much he could learn, if only he didn't have to go to school!

Well, at least the wheels had been set in motion. Once

he graduated, he'd have plenty of time for his investigations—maybe the University of Chicago would even *pay* him to come and do his experiments there. He had to get out. Had to get out. It was only the end of his first semester, and somehow he felt as if he'd lived two whole years since September.

13   Face-to-Face with Pu

Glory to Greg—it was he who had cautioned Conte to be sure to fill out two applications to take the qualifying exam for geometry. After that, everything followed in due course. On the day of the test Conte had merely picked up two test forms and used carbon paper. Thus, both his selves had been given credit for passing the qualifying exam. As a result, when Conte and Greg met to plan strategy for the spring semester, they discovered to their surprise that *Mark Conte #3449*, somehow, did not have to attend any regular classes at all!

"How'd we do it?" Greg shook his head violently.

"It's amazing!" Conte gazed at the schedules, still taped to the door of Greg's closet. "Coach Brown said I don't have to swim first period since I'm on the track team, so I've got first period *free*."

"And second period is algebra," added Greg, "which you don't have to take since you passed the exam . . ."

"I could choose to take geometry," Conte said, "or just have second period free."

Mr. Dean, his third period biology teacher, excused *Mark Conte* from class to work on the pyramid study.

Fourth period was free because another art project wasn't due until June.

In fifth period, Mr. Morse was giving him HIC history credit for a full report of the pyramid study.

This left only sixth period English with Mrs. Aherne. She happened also to be sponsor of the school newspaper, which needed a photographer for after-school sports events. Conte volunteered. In exchange for English credit, he would take photographs at the events that he usually had to attend anyhow, either as a member of the track team or the band. In a pinch, Greg would help him out. That meant during sixth period he was virtually free.

The two of them sat silently for a moment, awed at what they had achieved without even trying.

"Of course," Conte said, "there's still the other me. First period, study hall, I just sign in as before. I'll go to second period history with Miss Sommers. Third period HIC English with Gireaux—guess I'll spend that time reading in the library. Fourth period is band, and fifth period . . ."

"You finished algebra."

"Fifth period I'm signing up for geometry, and last

period is biology with Available Worfenstein. Greg, I've got it made. This is fantastic. I even have time to take an extra class if I want to . . ."

So the new idea originated. It germinated, then took hold.

"I'm going to take computer science myself, *this year*," Conte announced, and for once Greg was in full agreement.

"Sounds good," he said. "By next year you might be too busy; and you'll need that course to learn how to mess up Pu. You could work it in during first period, couldn't you."

"Yeah. And suppose Mr. Kelly didn't teach it next year for some reason. A person has to plan ahead, be prepared, get ready. . . ." Good grief, he was sounding like Greg!

Greg stretched and yawned and said, "You might have a slight problem. Mr. Kelly doesn't usually take freshmen."

"Maybe he'll take me. Besides—there will be two of us going to see him together. Me and Charlotta Jones."

"I don't think he likes girls, either."

"Everybody likes Charlotta. We'll go see him . . ."

"How? He's never out of that computer room, except for lunchtime. He eats in the cafeteria."

"What? That madhouse? You mean I have to see him in the *cafeteria*?"

"I guess so," said Greg. "Unless you want to go through your counselor, and that's risky. It could lead to all sorts of questions."

"I only went inside that cafeteria once," Conte said with a shiver.

It took Conte several days to get up his courage and to plan his attack. He knew all about Gladys Hutchinson, and that would help. But the cafeteria itself was another matter. One could only compare it to a hand-to-hand combat zone in ancient times, when the clash of sabers and the screams of men and cavalry horses rent the air.

No teacher would ever take noon duty in the cafeteria. Of course, noon duty was assigned. But the last time a teacher walked into the cafeteria during noontime, she was carried out on a stretcher. The teachers therefore had an unspoken agreement to totally ignore lunchtime and noon duty. They customarily ate their lunches at a little hamburger joint several blocks away.

So, in the cafeteria it was every man for himself, and Mr. Gordon Kelly was the only full-grown man there. He adored watching food being served up by Mrs. Gladys Hutchinson. He also adored eating the leftovers that could no longer be converted into hash, soup, or that sobering concoction called "Saturday stew." Mr. Gordon Kelly ate a lot and never got fatter, since he expended enormous energy worrying about Pu.

Mrs. Gladys Hutchinson, however, weighed two hundred and thirty pounds if she weighed an ounce. Everybody knew Mrs. Hutchinson and her obsession. She was a women's libber of the first order; she insisted upon calling herself "Ms" and pronounced it "Muzz."

It was "Muzz" Hutchinson's self-appointed task to give out lectures along with lunch. She cited herself as an example of a woman who had "escaped the tyranny of the kitchen."

"Getcher an education, gal," she'd say vehemently, scooping up a whopping portion of macaroni and cheese. "No other way you'll get out of the kitchen, hon."

The boys, too, were handed her message, along with their ice cream. "Listen, sonny, when you get married, don't look for your wife to stay home with nothing better to do than mend your socks and feed your face. A woman wants to get out in the world—be a 'muzz' instead of a 'missus'—want a piece of pie to go under that ice cream, son?"

"Muzz" Hutchinson was so busy with her duties and her lectures, that she seemed oblivious to the noontime chaos. As the crush subsided, she'd lean over the counter watching Mr. Gordon Kelly eat to his heart's content. When the crowd thinned, she'd come out and join him at the table, enticing him. "We've got half a dozen cold tacos left over from yesterday, Mr. Gordon Kelly. Shall I get them for you?"

"Oh, my dear 'Muzz' Hutchinson, I simply couldn't. Just make it three or four."

It was while Mr. Gordon Kelly was munching his cold tacos and looking forward to chocolate pudding afterward, that Conte and Charlotta approached him.

Conte said, "Mr. Kelly, may we speak to you for a moment, please?"

Mr. Gordon Kelly nodded and invited them to be seated. Mrs. Hutchinson stood by, beaming.

Charlotta said hello to "Muzz" Hutchinson and expressed regret at not being able to eat in the cafeteria more often.

"Mr. Kelly, we'd like to study computer science with you," Conte began. "I've got first period free, and Charlotta and I . . ."

"What year are you in?" Crumbs fell from Mr. Kelly's mouth while he spoke.

"Freshman, sir, but I learn fast, and I'm very mechanical." Conte glanced around, seeking some object upon which to prove his mechanical ability. He found only the napkin holder, and proceeded to take it apart while he spoke.

"A computer," said Mr. Kelly, "is not a toy."

Conte turned to Mrs. Hutchinson. She stood with her arms folded, unmoved.

Charlotta said softly, "I do think that girls ought to be allowed to develop their mechanical ability, don't you, Mr. Kelly? It's so important for them."

Conte said, "Mr. Kelly, I'll work hard. I'll learn fast. Please, please Mr. Kelly. I've been reading about computers ever since I was seven. Have you read *Computer Terminals and their Hook-ups*? Terrific book. I'll lend it to you. Oh, of course you know, *Circuits and Switches, a Basic Guide . . .*"

"Young man," said Mr. Kelly sternly, dropping taco crumbs again, "go away and leave me in peace."

"Mr. Kelly, Charlotta won't take the course unless I do. She wants to learn computer programming. She's a hard worker, and a nice girl. . . ."

"But," said Mr. Kelly, "I don't need anymore students. I've got enough to do."

"Charlotta just wants to learn something," Conte said, "so she can get a job and make something of herself. She doesn't just want to sit home and be a housewife. I could help her learn, because I know technology, but poor Charlotta, she never had a chance to learn stuff like that. She's always been too busy. She's got four little brothers, and her mother makes her do all the laundry!"

"Young man!" Gordon Kelly said angrily.

"Muzz" Hutchinson braced herself against the table. She gave Mr. Gordon Kelly a certain stare. He winced. It was settled very rapidly, with no misunderstanding. For the sake of a few stale tacos and some leftover pudding, Mr. Gordon Kelly would bend. Well, stronger men have bent for less.

Thus Charlotta Jones and Mark Conte were enrolled in computer science. For the first three days they were indoctrinated with Mr. Gordon Kelly's CODE:

1. In all matters of conflict, crisis, or question THE COMPUTER COMES FIRST.

2. Temperature in the computer room must at all times remain at the constant level of 68°F.

3. No equipment, cards, or tapes shall leave the computer room without authorization.

4. GARBAGE IN—GARBAGE OUT.

Conte and Charlotta then began to learn how a computer really works—how it is programmed, maintained, serviced, used. Within a month Mr. Kelly was letting them work out simple computer programs, just for practice. It was the sort of special class Conte had always longed for, with only eight students altogether, and each working at his own pace.

The work was difficult. It required great concentration. But with it came a feeling of tremendous pride. One little card could mold the destiny of millions! It was thrilling to contemplate the marvels that could be achieved with an obedient machine.

If only he didn't have to go to school! Conte would happily have spent every day, all day, in the computer room. Well, he'd get out soon enough, go on to college, where perhaps he could devote all his time to programming a computer to record and analyze the results of his pyramid experiments. Oh, he could go on forever punching cards, checking codes, redesigning systems. And he was good at it. Mr. Gordon Kelly often said so.

As for Charlotta, after several weeks she confessed to Conte, "This just isn't my bag. But I'll stick it out and just do what you tell me."

Charlotta's submissive willingness to let Conte be the boss, gave him a fabulous idea. He would program the computer *now*, to graduate him next year, after each of his selves had completed seventy-two units. He'd get everything ready, feed his instructions into the computer, then simply sit back and wait until next year. Because by next year, who could tell? Maybe he wouldn't be so fortunate as to have a good friend like Charlotta Jones, who was a nice girl but not adverse to cheating a little when it came to helping out a friend.

The good thing about a computer is that you can program it way ahead of time. A computer doesn't mind waiting. It'll do what you tell it, when you tell it to, and it never asks why. Conte began to understand why Mr. Gordon Kelly felt tender toward Pu. Pu did as it was told, with no hassle. Not many humans—or even animals—can make that claim.

In programming a computer, one must be precise. A single mistake, and the whole thing turns out "garbage." "Garbage" is *never* the fault of the computer, unless it is

Mr. Gordon Kelly himself who has personally designed the program. Then if something goes wrong, Mr. Gordon Kelly speaks of "inherent mechanical error," and sometimes he gives Pu a good swift kick in the side.

For Conte to design a program by which Pu would automatically graduate him after two years was no easy task. About twenty-three steps would be involved. Portions of the program would have to be tested. That was where Charlotta came in. She could be counted upon (with no questions asked) to keep Mr. Kelly occupied and out of the computer room, at least for a few minutes at a time.

Obviously, Conte couldn't redesign the entire computer system for the school. He had to learn the system and take advantage of its existing procedures. Basically, the computer worked like this:

When a student had completed 144 units of work, the computer would segregate that student's card. The cards were assembled, and the names on the cards were printed onto a master list of students eligible to graduate. Conte's basic plan was to get his name on that list at the proper time. How could it be accomplished?

Each semester the computer automatically scanned the cards and filed them according to units completed. Thus it separated freshmen, sophomores, juniors, and seniors. Once in a while a student skipped a year by going to summer school or taking extra courses. That was why each card was scanned every term, a project that takes only a few minutes for a computer.

Conte's main task was to instruct the computer to combine the total unit credits on the separate cards for Conte Mark and *Mark Conte*. Timing was vital. The credits on the two cards had to be combined *after* each card had registered 72 units. Thus, instructions to the computer would go something like this:

When card ⫟3449 shows a total of 72 units, seek out card ⫟3762, combine the totals of the two cards onto card ⫟3762, and release card ⫟3449. Conte would be waiting to catch and dispose of card ⫟3449. It would then appear as if *Mark Conte* had never existed. The computer, having added the credits together, would immediately proceed to add the name, Conte Mark, to the master list of graduates.

It sounded simple. But such a plan requires logic, precise planning, and hard work. Night after night Conte sat up late working out his computer program. If only he could try it out on a dry run! Impossible. Like a bank robbery, it would have to be a now-or-never, one shot deal.

At night, having finished his work, Conte would sit on the floor polishing his trophy. The slow, steady motion helped him relax. It didn't keep him from worrying. It just made him feel relaxed while he was worrying. And he had plenty to worry about.

Should anything really go wrong with the computer,

Mr. Gordon Kelly, usually as mild as a well-fed orangu-
tang in the zoo, became ferocious. Twice before it had
happened. A major error in the computer had occurred,
and one of the students was deemed responsible. The
name of that particular student was spoken only in whispers after that.

What Mr. Kelly did when the computer "cracked
up," was to shut everything down completely. Then he
went over the entire mechanism with a fine-tooth-comb.
Woe to the person who was even remotely responsible
for jamming Pu's sensitive circuits! Poor Mr. Gordon
Kelly! When such an ordeal was over, he was always in
such a state of nervous exhaustion that he had to be hos-
pitalized for a week.

Therefore, Conte had good cause to worry. He certainly didn't want to make any mistakes. He didn't want
to cause a complete shut-down and subsequent fine-
tooth-comb inquiry. An inquiry would surely show that
somebody had been tampering with the machine; and
among the student helpers in the computer room, there
were few to choose from. Lastly, Conte didn't want to
be responsible for putting Mr. Kelly in the hospital.

Mr. Gordon Kelly had many idiosyncrasies. He was
stubborn. He was unreasonable. He was a fanatic. But
Conte understood him perfectly and even liked him. In
fact, Conte was beginning to get the uneasy feeling that
in some ways he was a whole lot like Mr. Gordon Kelly.

14 "My Boy"

Conte's worries were not confined to school. They sometimes began even before school. Like the morning his mother got up early and fixed his breakfast. Two eggs, she gave him, toast, bacon, and oatmeal. What had gotten into her?

"I can't eat all that," Conte grumbled. "Leave me alone."

"How about some French toast, then? Drink your milk."

"Mom, I don't even have time to eat all this stuff. Why'd you get up, anyway? I always get my own breakfast. You know I don't like to talk in the morning."

She was hurt. She sniffed, hard, stomped out of the kitchen and went to her "garret." She proceeded to bang away so hard that even the light fixture in the kitchen vibrated.

Back again, hands on hips, she confronted him. "So, don't eat the eggs. See if I care. You can't even seem to find time to spend a half hour doing that wiring I've been asking you about."

"I'll do it tomorrow!"

"You did it tomorrow last month," she said.

"I'll do it today!" he yelled.

"Forget it. I'll do it myself. I refuse to be dependent upon a person who can't even eat two fried eggs for breakfast!"

Greg was late. He'd been up half the night, he said, with his mother, watching the hatching of the eggs of the yellow-headed jawfish from the Florida reefs. Also, he was low on gas. They had to coast down into the school parking lot, already late, and because he was tardy, Conte had to parry with Mr. Gireaux.

Usually the students paired up. Whoever was left worked with Mr. Gireaux. It was unnerving, for Mr. Gireaux liked to carry on an animated conversation while he lunged and thrusted, twirled and finally touched. Each touch was a point against one's opponent, and four touches won the game.

Usually Mr. Gireaux confined his comments, while fencing, to pleasantries about the weather. But with Conte, because he was a HIC English student, things went further.

"What do you suppose," Mr. Gireaux asked, lunging,

"was the condition of women in Shakespeare's time; what motivated him to write *The Taming of the Shrew*?"

"Uh?" Conte took two defensive steps backward, executed a very ungraceful half-turn, only to be met on the right by his teacher's blade, accompanied by the question, "How would you compare the domestic problems of Hamlet and King Richard III?"

Conte valiantly tried to answer, but Mr. Gireaux executed a *fleche*, and somehow Conte was sent sprawling.

It is quite undignified to be knocked down during a gentlemanly fencing match with one's teacher—especially when at the moment of impact a mechanical device that has been strapped to one's chest begins to emit strange noises.

"What is the matter, my boy?" Mr. Gireaux was flustered. "Are you ill?"

"No, no," said Conte, dusting himself off. "It's just my gadget."

"Gadget?" In that moment the plastic cover came off the device lent to Conte by Mr. Dean—a device that measured heartbeat. It rolled across the floor.

"Oh, it's not *part* of me," Conte explained, for obviously Mr. Gireaux imagined that Conte was being kept alive by some surgical hardware implanted in his chest, which he, Mr. Gireaux, had just knocked loose.

"I'm fine," Conte insisted, as Mr. Gireaux continued

to stare. "This is just for my biology experiment."

"One should not," said Mr. Gireaux, "do too many things at once."

Too many things at once? Absurd. Apparently Mr. Gireaux had never heard of Leonardo DaVinci, and didn't respect the qualities of flexibility and versatility. He, Conte Mark, could do plenty of things at once. Plenty.

During first period Conte walked down to Katz Beach to work on his experiments. (Computer science class was cancelled for Pu's annual oiling.) Even from fifty yards away Conte could tell something was wrong. Somebody—a whole mess of somebodies—had been fooling around with his pyramid.

People had written words onto the side of it with pen or crayon or charcoal. One of the words was SID, which isn't bad in itself, but the word following was of dubious caliber. Someone, too, had decided to use the pyramid for messages. (The hanging tree was less convenient.) One was scrawled in paint, "Murray, meet me here tomorrow night at 8." Another person had had the gall to stick a thumb tack into the pyramid, bearing the notice, "For Sale: Three Book Reports." Somebody else with an artistic flair had painted a very large red and purple eye near the apex of the pyramid. All in all, it was a mess.

At least inside everything was intact, Conte thought,

investigating his work table and various objects set there to absorb pyramid power. No—things were not OK. The jar containing the multitude of snails had been knocked over, and dozens of little snails were stuck onto the pyramid's inner walls. And under Conte's file box was the most significant piece of evidence that some-body had been misappropriating his pyramid: a sign such as one finds in motels, DO NOT DISTURB, and under it somebody had printed the word, TESTING.

Conte angrily tore up the sign and, from a piece of notebook paper made one of his own, KEEP OUT OR ELSE! It was getting so a person couldn't even have the privacy of his own pyramid! Rotten town, rotten school, rotten bunch of crooks—breaking into a person's property! He couldn't wait to get out of this place and never see any of them again. Except, maybe for Pamela. And Mr. Mott. And—well, he wouldn't mind keeping track of Flint and Charlotta, and maybe coming back to say hello to Gordon Kelly and Available Worfenstein. . . .

Conte had every intention of going to class the rest of that day. Vaguely he recalled that for some reason it was an important day. Friday, March twelfth. During sec-ond period he went to history with Miss Sommers. Dur-ing third period he checked briefly with Mr. Dean on his biology projects. Mr. Dean repaired the heartbeat device and recommended some further experiments with it, both inside and outside the pyramid.

"Try jogging both inside and outside the pyramid," he said, "and note whether there are any differences in your pulse and heartbeat."

Conte planned to spend a few minutes during the remainder of third period doing just that. But Pamela appeared on the path just as he was leaving Mr. Dean's room. She approached him and came right to the point.

"Conte," she said, "let's go down to Katz Beach."

"But Pamela, you've got class, haven't you?"

"Let's go down to Katz Beach."

"Pamela, don't you think? . . ."

"Conte, take me to Katz Beach."

He sighed, and they began to walk together. They walked for several minutes without speaking. Then Pamela said, "I want to sit in your pyramid and learn to tell my right hand from my left."

"Pamela, what makes you think the pyramid can do that? Listen, I'm beginning to think that maybe this whole pyramid power thing is just a gimmick. . . ."

"We'll try it," Pamela said. "I have been hearing fabulous things about the pyramid."

"For instance?"

"For instance, how Flint got goals. How Charlotta's even going straight—she hasn't done a thing wrong since that dummy episode. And Miss Worfenstein's getting married . . ."

"What? What's my pyramid got to do with Available

Worfenstein? Who would want to marry her? How do you know so much?"

"Miss Worfenstein," said Pamela calmly, "has been using your pyramid. I know, because I've been down here wanting to use it myself. I saw her in it."

"With . . . ?"

"Alone. I knew it was Miss Worfenstein. I heard her laughing. Then she came out, alone. She'd been sitting in there reading a magazine—laughing—and getting the power."

"The—the power?"

"Mr. Mott proposed to her the following day. Ask anybody. All the kids know."

"*I* didn't know."

"You—you're always disappearing. How can you know anything that goes on?"

"I know plenty! I know everything I need to know!"

"Then teach me," Pamela said softly, "to tell my right hand from my left."

They had walked all the way down to where the pyramid stood. "What's happened to your pyramid, Conte?" Pamela spoke in a whisper.

"Graffiti," Conte whispered back. "It's OK. I was mad before, but now—I think I'll just use it for my art project. Very modern."

"I didn't know you took art!"

"Shh."

They went inside and sat down on the cushion, close together. Sunlight filtered in, an amber glow between the cracks in the cardboard. It was strangely like being in the secluded belfry of a church with stained glass windows. Colors here in the pyramid were mellow and muted. It was warm—lazily and pleasantly warm. A lassitude came over Conte, a delicious sleepiness. Slowly, softly, soothingly, Pamela began to talk.

Never before had they had so much time to talk. So much time away from everything and everybody. So much time for Conte just to listen while Pamela talked and talked about her parents, each of whom was trying to push her into a different career, and her three brothers taking sides first with one, then the other.

"I want to fly more than anything in the world!" Pamela's eyes were wide and intense. "My mother wants me to be a stewardess. But I want to be a pilot! My dad's the only one who takes my side. It's awful. They're all pulling me in different directions, and I just don't know —why can't they just leave me alone?"

Conte only grunted.

"I want to make my own decisions! But how can I? As long as I can't even tell my right hand from my left . . . listen, I couldn't even tie my shoes until I was seven. I have terrible coordination."

"False," said Conte. "You play the flute. That takes coordination."

"But when it comes to mechanical things—I'm a washout. Of course, until I get better at things like that, I really don't *have* to choose, do I." She stopped and stared at Conte. "Did you hear what I just said?"

"Yes."

"Do you understand what that means?"

"I think so."

"Conte, people are right about this pyramid! Do you know why I haven't been able to learn to tell right from left? Because when I do learn, I'll have to face my problem. I'll have to make a choice. But if I never learn, I'll avoid that conflict. Well," she said determinedly, "I *will* learn. Tell me, Conte, is this my right hand?"

"No, it's your left."

"Then this is the right. Right. Right. Conte," she said, "please kiss me."

"What?"

"Kiss me."

He did.

She held up her right hand. "Again."

And so Pamela—wisely recognizing that when a correct response is rewarded a person learns very rapidly—Pamela proceeded to solicit kisses to firmly imprint upon her brain the fact that right is right and left is left. For Conte, it represented a whole new dimension in education.

Time—what is time when the day is an amber glow,

the sound of the surf whispers in your ears, and the air is so fresh that you can almost subsist on it alone? There's nobody to bother you or tell you what must be done—in the pyramid it is peaceful and quiet. . . ."

"Oh! What time is it?" Conte jumped up, ran out of the pyramid, leaped up again in alarm. "Did you hear that? Pamela! Do you hear that? It's the band! The loudspeakers! Pamela, it's Friday the twelfth, and we must have been here for *hours*. . . ."

"So what? We didn't do anything. . . ."

"The track meet, that's so what!" He began to run, and Pamela ran along side him. "I'm running in the track meet. Oh, oh," he moaned. "I promised Mrs. Aherne we'd get photos of the meet. I was supposed to get Greg to do it. Oh, oh," he moaned again, "Mr. Mott wanted me to play the saxophone solo. We're playing at half time. I'll never make it," he cried, panting as he ran up the hill. "I can't do it. There isn't three of me."

"No," said Pamela. "Only two."

Conte stopped, stared at her, gasping, "What? What did you say?"

"I've known it for a long time," Pamela said calmly.

"And you haven't told?"

"Listen," she said, grinning, "if a person wants to be two persons and doesn't want to tell the other person, what right has the other person to tell third persons about the person that's being two persons?"

"Pamela, I've got to go to the track meet."

"I'll come and watch you run. I'll listen to you play. And you can take my picture," she said.

If it had not been for those peaceful hours in the pyramid, Conte would never have survived the rest of that afternoon. Coach Brown was furious that Conte was late for the meet. Mr. Mott was very angry when Conte jumped into his place with the band, wearing his track suit. Too dry-mouthed to perform, Conte managed to squeeze a few husky squeaks out of his instrument before he was banned from the group. To save something of the day, Conte grabbed his camera to get a good shot of the high jump. So unique was the angle, that as he clicked the shutter, the jumper nearly landed on Conte's head.

At last the afternoon was over. Greg had long since gone home, so Conte walked. The hill seemed to become ever steeper. His breathing was labored. When at last Conte walked in the front door, his entire body was wet with sweat.

"Hey, Conte! Look here—I've done it." His mother stood there in the living room with a contraption the likes of which Conte had never seen before.

It was—what was it? It was a conglomeration of old auto parts, stove parts, hardware from the store, odd-sized handles of brass, steel, chrome. It was—what was it? It was about five and a half feet tall, with two long

appendages like arms, a pedestal instead of feet, but with
toes, twelve of them in all. It had a head—oh, what a
head!—with too many mouths and noses and not enough
eyes, and it had buttons all over, buttons on its belly,
buttons on its chest and on its rear.

It was—what was it? Conte's mother gave a broad
grin. "Ta-daa!" she sang. "Now," she proclaimed, "now
for the *coup de gras!*" She flipped a switch or pressed a
button, and that thing began to wriggle and jiggle,
shimmy and shake. Its arms flapped and clattered. Buttons went ping and zing and buzz. The head wobbled
and turned clear around, turned back again, and something kept clapping, clapping like cymbals. Conte was
stunned. A moment later he saw the small engraved plate
welded onto the pedestal, bearing the title of the work.
Conte stared. It said MY BOY. And in that moment MY
BOY gave one last shudder and began, literally, to fall
apart.

It was not a complimentary statement. His own mother
saw him as a crazy mixed-up nut who rattled and flapped
like a machine, who spun his head clear around in a
circle, accomplished nothing, made weird noises. His
own mother thought he was nothing but a bunch of
buttons and switches, a person without brains, without
goals, without feelings.

"How'd she think I'd feel?" Conte exclaimed, talking to Pamela on the telephone. "You should have seen that hunk of junk. It rattled all over, and then it fell apart. She's trying to tell me something. I know her. She thinks she's so subtle. She's telling me that I'm falling apart."

Pamela said, "I think she just doesn't know how to wire things and that's why it fell apart."

"No. She planned it that way. My mom's very devious. Once when I came home from school, she was dressed in a prison suit. I don't know where she got it. Why do you think she was dressed in a prison suit? To impress upon me that I was supposed to make my own bed and clean my room. She said she was a prisoner, a prisoner of the house, because nobody helped her. Can you beat that?"

"Your mother," said Pamela, "sounds fascinating."

"She's a kook. Listen, I'm just glad I'm getting out of here next . . ."

He stopped abruptly. He had no intention of confiding his whole plan to Pamela. Trust nobody, that was his motto. He'd already taken a chance trusting Greg, but that was a necessity.

There followed a long silence. Then Pamela said, "Well, I'd better get off the phone now."

That, too, stung him. He asked coldly, "Don't you want to know what I mean about getting out of here? Don't you care to know where I'm going?"

"Conte," said Pamela sweetly, "I don't believe that a person should meddle in the business of another person if that person . . ."

"Cut it out!" he yelled.

"I am not a snoop," Pamela said. "Whatever you do is OK. You don't need to explain." Then, talking very fast she said, "I love you anyhow," and then she hung up.

15 Some Shocks and Surprises

A change had come over Available Worfenstein. For one thing, she now did make herself available to counsel the students. But she was also different in other ways. Her laugh was softer, more refined. She still talked animatedly, but she spoke less.

The change in Mr. Mott was exactly the opposite. Where before he had been hesitant and silent, acquiescent and meek, he now began to assert himself. He laughed more. He talked more. And he put his foot down about a few things. Wonder of wonders—it turned out that Mr. Mott, too, had paid several secret visits to Conte's pyramid.

"Of course, there is a marvelous source of power in that pyramid," Mr. Mott told Conte, "though it has nothing to do with the shape, as far as I can tell."

Conte nodded. "It's our society," he said. "Our whole culture. The Mexicans take *siesta*. Indians meditate.

What do we do? We rush and chase and hurry. That's why we can't think straight."

"That's true," said Mr. Mott. "I went inside your pyramid because Miss Worfenstein told me how relaxing it was. Actually, she started using it for quite a different purpose."

"What was that?" Conte asked.

Mr. Mott smiled. "She thought it would curl her hair. She found out it didn't do anything to her hair. But it did do something for her—for her inner life, as she told me. Those were her very words. A quietude came over her, she said. Well," Mr. Mott coughed slightly, hesitated momentarily, then smiled again. "I began to see Miss Worfenstein the way she really is. I—we are going to be married in June. You shall, of course, be invited to the wedding. After all, it was your pyramid that did it."

Mr. Mott continued. "I decided to try your pyramid. I went down and sat in it several times during lunch break. While I sat there, I began to reflect on many things. I grew sleepy, but I wasn't really asleep. I was just far away, I guess, into my own thoughts. I began to think about my life, my students, the band."

Mr. Mott raised himself up very straight, and he looked at Conte intently. "We've got a pretty good band at Vista Mar High," he said.

"Yes, sir, we do."

"But it's not going to be just 'pretty good' anymore,

Conte. While I was sitting in your pyramid, I realized that I haven't been quite fair to the band. Some members," he said, "have been getting away with murder. Next year it's going to be different. I will accept no excuses for people missing rehearsals. When it comes to office work, I've told Mr. Granberg I intend to use the paid secretarial staff and not my students. I hear that Charlotta Jones is going to graduate this June. That's fine. Because I'm not going to allow people to be in band just taking up space anymore. Don't get me wrong, Charlotta's a nice girl, but she really isn't interested in music. From now on, we're going to have more than a 'pretty good' band. We're going to have a great band. And we're all going to work."

Conte stared at Mr. Mott. His pyramid—his pyramid had done all this? He knew exactly what was coming, and mentally he braced himself for it.

"Now, if you want to be my assistant," Mr. Mott continued, "and I do believe you have the capability to become student conductor, then you're going to have to make a choice. Band takes a lot of time. So does track. So does art. So does anything worthwhile. I'm not asking you to give up everything. But you're going to have to decide where you want to place your main emphasis. I sincerely hope you will choose the band."

With that statement, Mr. Mott turned and began to busy himself clearing the junk off the piano. One after the other he tossed items into a large carton—things like jackets and old, stale lunches and backless books. Thus Mr. Mott removed the trash that had for years accumulated in the band room, and Conte understood completely the symbolic nature of this sudden clean-up spree.

It had to be done before spring vacation. After spring vacation the computer room became as busy as a termite mound after a storm. After spring vacation, the computer had to print out promotion sheets, make up class lists for next term, prepare graduation lists, and get ready for the incoming freshmen.

So Conte's program had to be put in now, before the big rush, before Charlotta graduated, and before Mr. Gordon Kelly got suspicious.

Why should Mr. Kelly get suspicious? Because Conte spent an inordinate amount of time in the computer room. These moments always coincided with times when Charlotta Jones waylaid Mr. Kelly on some absurd pretext. Charlotta—even ingenious Charlotta Jones—was just about running out of excuses. She had used quite a few:

"Mr. Kelly—see that bright light over there? Could it be a flying saucer?"

"Mr. Kelly, I think I'm going to faint."

"Oh, Mr. Kelly, I saw a rattlesnake over by the side of the building!"

"Mr. Kelly! Mr. Kelly! 'Muzz' Hutchinson wants you in the cafeteria!"

Naturally, Conte took all possible opportunities to test out portions of his program. So far, the separate parts were satisfactory. Thus it was with an air of confidence that Conte, on the day before spring vacation, persuaded Charlotta to perform her final and most spectacular bit of dramatics. Her assignment: to keep Mr. Gordon Kelly out of the computer room for ten whole minutes.

Charlotta was willing to do it—for a price.

"I don't have anything you want," Conte objected.

"Oh, yes, you do."

"Well, whatever it is, you can't have it."

"Everybody," said Charlotta, "has his price."

"What do you want?"

"Your pyramid."

"Why do you want that? I'm not going to give you my pyramid. It cost me . . ."

"I didn't say 'give.' I mean to buy it from you," said Charlotta.

"But you can buy one from the Comminger Catalogue Company," Conte said. "Why do you need mine?"

"Yours is broken in," Charlotta replied. "It's tried and tested. A new one might not have the same power."

"I'm not through with it. . . ."

"You will be, by June. I'll take it then."

"I wouldn't sell my pyramid for anything, it's . . ."

"I'll give you fifty dollars."

"Sold!"

So it was all arranged. After graduation, Charlotta would take possession of the pyramid. In return, she would give Conte fifty dollars and guarantee him at least fifteen minutes in the computer room without Mr. Gordon Kelly. Just how Charlotta planned to accomplish this, Conte did not inquire. He was sure, however, that she had ways.

Now, a computer is a delicate and sensitive device. One must approach it a certain way, talk to it, if you will, in its own language. Conte, who had a inborn flair for all things mechanical, had no qualms about making the computer do his bidding.

On that unforgettable day in April, Conte awoke with a song in his heart and a cold in his head. Or, perhaps it was hayfever. Whatever the cause, he felt simultaneously thrilled and wrung out. Dag's moaning and howling had awakened him several times in the night. His nose was stuffed. His head felt heavy. Still, he was as excited as a little kid on his birthday morning.

As if she knew something was afoot, his mom met him in the kitchen. "Morning," she said curtly. "Want some cocoa?"

"Sure." So, he'd do her a favor. Let her make cocoa for him. After all, she was his mother. He still had not quite gotten over her "contraption," but one had to make allowances for mothers who are artists.

"Got a cold?"

"Hayfever."

"Think it comes from not sleeping or eating properly? Conte, honey," she said earnestly, sitting down at the table with him, "I worry about you."

"Me? Why worry about me? I'm just the old mechanical man. Flip, flop, rattle, clatter . . ."

"Conte, I meant it as. . . . I had no idea it would hurt your feelings. Honey, you've got to understand something about art. An artistic statement isn't always . . ."

"Mom, I've got to hurry. Tell me about it some other time."

She glared at him, but held her ground. Silently she sipped her coffee. Then she remarked, "Dag howled again. It's driving me nuts. But at least I found out what's bugging him."

"You did? What is it?"

"A poodle."

"What do you mean?"

"Female poodle. Down the street. In heat now. Every few months—well, now we know."

"You mean Dag's in love with a poodle? A little poodle?"

"Well, Conte, I wouldn't exactly say 'in love.' But he certainly is restless."

"Well, why don't you just let him out?"

"I did," said his mother. "I even met the woman who owns the poodle. A Mrs. Bleaker. Funny—she looks something like the poodle herself—curly hair, beady eyes, undershot jaw. She's very nice. She even said Dag was welcome at their house. I explained we're all having trouble sleeping, you see. She said as far as she was concerned, Dag could come over and sleep with the poodle in the garage."

"Let him, then."

"I tried. The poodle rejected Dag. It's a very conceited little dog—got a pedigree, I guess. Wears a hair ribbon. Anyhow, it made Dag feel rotten. He just came slinking home and started to howl in the afternoon. You'd know, if you were ever home."

"I am ever home! Just because I didn't have time to wire your—your *junk*. . . ."

Suddenly she was crying. Her eyes were red rimmed. And Conte knew those tears had nothing to do with sorrow. She was simply outraged.

"I'm sorry! I'm sorry!" he called, fleeing. He ran back, grabbed his notebook. "I'm sorry. I'll see you this afternoon. *Don't be so mad*."

Well, that was how she was; you could say almost anything to his Mom. She wasn't square or mean or old-fashioned. But say something uncomplimentary about her art, and—watch out. Supper tonight would be frozen tamales, still soggy, and lime jello. You could bank on that. If they were very lucky, she'd give them a tossed salad. More likely she'd fix something really revolting like persimmon and raw fig salad with French dressing. She had done that last year when Dad said her sculpture of the three presidents looked like a pine cone and two balloons.

He heard Greg's horn and jumped into the car. "Today's the day!" Conte said gleefully. "*My* day. I'm gonna plant that little old program of mine smack inside that smarty computer, and next year at this time— whoopee! Hey, do you realize that you and I will graduate together?"

"Terrific," said Greg. Since the hatching of the yellow-headed jawfish from the Florida reefs, Greg seldom repeated himself anymore. In fact, he had become rather curt.

They went to fencing class. Then afterward, like a doctor preparing for surgery, Conte went to scrub his hands, and with a meaningful nod to Charlotta, proceeded into the computer room.

Alone at last with Pu, Conte simply stood there, savoring the tremendous feeling of awe that precedes any grand and noble undertaking. So must Alexander Graham Bell have felt just before he lifted the receiver and called, "Watson, I want you!"

Actually, it was almost anti-climatic. The whole thing was accomplished in less than two minutes. All Conte had to do was insert the program card he had devised, and press a single button.

There was an almost inaudible hum, lasting only a fraction of a second. Then it was all over. Conte's heart was pounding madly. His throat felt dry, his knees weak. He sat down on the floor. He looked up at the wall clock. Only three minutes had passed. Now the die had been cast. There was nothing more to do but to mind his business, go home and enjoy spring vacation, keep up the same pace next year, and then, oh joy, pack up for Chicago.

In the first week of May, Conte received two surprises that were really more in the nature of traumatic shocks.

Next to Vista Mar, in the town of Arlington Hills, was a small but influential art colony. Said colony annually sponsored an art show. Of course, Conte knew nothing of this, being a stranger to the world of art. All he did know was that one Sunday morning as he skimmed the newspaper, he suddenly came upon a photograph of his own mother. In the background stood that horrible heap titled MY BOY.

VISTA MAR WOMAN WINS ART PRIZE, said the caption. There followed an elaborate article about his mother, Constance Mark, who "manages to combine motherhood and sculpture with astonishing aplomb," with the added information that "her husband, Robert Mark, is a flexible man, but insists upon supper at seven each night."

Now Conte knew exactly why his mother had not mentioned the article. She hated the "woman artist" bit. More than one newspaper editor had been sent cowering into his office under the force of her attack. "Why do people insist on calling me a *mother* who happens to be an artist? How would you like it if you were introduced as somebody's *father*, whose *hobby* is editing a newspaper? Why won't you tell what's important about *me*? Did you ask my opinion of pop art, of the world political situation, of the artist in society? You did not!"

Angry and embarrassed, his mother had obviously done her best to forget about the article completely. But why, Conte wondered, hadn't she even told him about the art show? Didn't she think he cared? What kind of mother is it who keeps her kid in the dark about a thing like that, who doesn't want to share anything? She was still mad, he supposed, because he hadn't done that wiring for her. Well, it was just like her to hold a grudge that way.

Like a faint buzzing in his ear came the inner whisper, Liar! He tried to ignore it, and the hiss that followed, You know she never keeps a grudge. That's you, not she.

Well, it was an awful embarrassment, having that thing displayed, that awful disorganized, disoriented, crazy thing called MY BOY. What would people think?

What people? buzzed the voice, and Conte brushed it aside, silenced it by beginning to whistle.

People would think—they'd think . . . What would they think?

The words seemed to pop out at him from the article, the passage given in quotes:

> To me the piece is a statement about my boy, not as people usually romanticize their children—not as part of me—but as an individual. You see, I wanted to show those qualities in him that I especially treasure. His independence. His versatility. He's got so many talents, my boy. True, he gets a little fragmented sometimes, but that's part of being a kid and trying to find yourself.

The article concluded, "When asked what her son thought of her art, Mrs. Mark replied, 'No Comment.'"

"Qualities that I treasure . . ." Hmmm. Conte whistled as loudly and as brightly as he could. Still, those words flashed back at him, "He's got so many talents, my boy." Wow. She really knew how to hurt a guy. How to make him feel like a heel. Wow.

But that was nothing compared to traumatic shock number two, which was delivered to Conte at precisely nine forty-seven on Monday morning, May third, by the inimitable Charlotta Jones, who approached him in her subtle style. "Gee, man, you really goofed this time. Whatever you did to that computer, you just better not let Mr. Gordon Kelly find out."

"What's wrong? What's wrong?"

"Well, for one thing, it's inoperative," said Charlotta, using Mr. Kelly's own term. "It just conked out this morning. Obviously, somebody did something wrong."

"But it wasn't me," Conte cried.

"How about that day before spring vacation," said Charlotta, "when you were in here alone. Did you check the temperature control to be sure the room stayed at 68°?"

"I—I refuse to answer," Conte said stoutly, "on the grounds that it might incriminate me. Anyhow, that was over two weeks ago. What would that have to do with a malfunction now?"

Icily Charlotta said, "You know computers aren't time bound. It's perfectly possible that what you did then is affecting Pu today."

Why was she so mad? Why was she so cool? Sweet, warm, obliging Charlotta had suddenly turned sour on him. Well, that's how people are. You try to be nice to them, be friendly, and for no reason they turn on you. Well, he didn't need 'em. He didn't need anybody. . . .

With a strange smirk on her face, Charlotta turned

and took a sheet of paper from the work table. With a flourish, she handed it to Conte, then stood back to watch, as a demolition expert stands back to witness the blast.

Conte looked at the paper. He looked at Charlotta. He felt his face grow cold, as if all the warmth and life in his body were draining out through his toes. He opened his mouth to proclaim his horror in loud profanity, but not a single sound came out. Speechless—he was speechless.

Charlotta Jones had just handed him the computer's official list of those persons who were to graduate from Vista Mar High School this coming June.

With a little smile that wasn't the least bit nice, Charlotta Jones said, "Guess whose name is on that list, Conte Mark."

16   Conte Leaves His Mark

As a little boy, Conte had had a passion for trains. He had pushed wooden blocks along the floor with "hoo-hoo-chug-chug" noises. He had gotten cardboard cartons from the store and sat in them playing engineer to his heart's content. His dad, noticing this obsession, naturally figured that the perfect Christmas gift would be an electric train. Right? Dead wrong.

On Christmas morning when Conte had seen the little electric train chugging around the Christmas tree, he had burst into tears. His father, being a flexible man, and a man who truly loved his son, understood. He packed the train away, gave Conte a hug and said, "I'm sorry, son. It was wrong of me. It's too much, too soon."

That was precisely how Conte felt when he saw his name on that list of graduates.

Since handing him the bombshell, Charlotta Jones had not moved a muscle. Now she said, with a toss of her head, "This is what happens when *amateurs* try to get out of their league."

"What—what do you mean?"

"You wrecked the computer, didn't you?"

Conte stared at her, speechless. Then, in a rush of clarity, he realized why she was behaving so coldly. She didn't mind him fooling with the computer. She didn't even mind him graduating early. Actually, for all she knew, he had purposely gotten his name on the list of graduates for this June. What Charlotta couldn't forgive was that she had not been consulted. He had used her help, without letting her in on the plan.

Now humbly he said (although humility did hurt), "Charlotta, I should have told you about it. Forgive me. You see, I made a mess of things. If only I'd asked you."

Charlotta gave a sniff and glanced down at her fingernails, trying to hide the slight smile that came creeping at the corners of her mouth.

"Charlotta, I must get into that computer room, just one more time. If you could arrange it for me . . ."

"What," she said coldly, "will you offer this time?"

"I will tell you the whole scheme, from the beginning," Conte said. "You see, I have made a mistake. I wasn't planning to graduate just yet. It all started . . ."

"Tell it, baby," Charlotta crooned, for she truly adored a good caper, and her curiosity was like an excruciating itch that demanded scratching. "Tell it," she murmured, and Conte did.

Conte told the whole story. Then he concluded, "Of course, I'm going to have to get my name off this list. I can't possibly graduate this June."

Charlotta's eyes were gleaming, and her breathing was erratic. "Why not, Conte?" she exclaimed. Suddenly all her movements were electric. She rushed to grasp his arm. "Why not? You'd be the talk of the school! Imagine, getting out of high school in just one year. You could go to the University of Chicago next fall. They've got some kids there even younger than you. And you're smart, Conte—really smart. Just think—you'd be off on your own. You'd go places, meet people, do terrific things. Why don't you just take that diploma now, Conte? It would be awful to waste a perfectly good diploma. Maybe," she crooned, "I'll apply to the University of Chicago, too. Wouldn't it be a blast if we both went there together? Maybe I could talk Flint into transferring there next year—oh, just think of the capers, the pranks, the tricks, the escapades . . ."

For a moment Conte almost imagined himself going along with it. But something about that last bit, "capers, the pranks, the tricks, the escapades," reminded him of Greg. It reminded him of the beginning of this whole affair. It had all seemed so logical, way back last September. But now—now things were different. He was perfectly willing to graduate a year from now. Perfectly willing. One year from now he'd have accomplished all he wanted here. He'd be ready to move on. But not quite yet.

Firmly Conte shook his head and said, "Charlotta, I can't do it. Not yet. It's too cold in Chicago. Why, I read they're expecting a record snow next winter. Nope. I'll have to get my name off that list somehow."

"Lotsa luck, Conte. With Mr. Gordon Kelly in this murderous mood, nobody will be able to get near that computer for weeks. By then it'll be too late. These lists are supposed to be distributed tomorrow."

"Distributed?"

"To all the people involved—the attendance office, the counselors, the principal, the district office."

"How many lists are there?"

"About a dozen."

Conte was silent for several moments. Then he said, "Charlotta, I have got to get into that computer room for a few minutes. Just once more, that's all I ask. Even two minutes will do it."

"Conte, I've just about run out of ideas. . . ."

"You? No," he said, "not you."

Charlotta nodded. "All right, Conte. Give me a couple of minutes. Then be ready to dash inside."

In a twinkling she was gone, and a few moments later an alarm sounded, and the shout went through the school, "Fire drill! Fire drill!"

When it was all over, and Conte had spent those last minutes with Pu, he kissed Charlotta soundly on the cheek. "I've got some heavy thinking to do," he said. "I might call you tonight."

He got Greg Gaff out of class. The two of them went to the office, faked double cases of food poisoning and headed for home. In Greg's room, they deliberated.

"What's happened?" Greg asked.

"Near as I can figure it," said Conte, "I made a slight mistake."

"That's obvious," Greg said scornfully.

"I had programmed the computer to add together the units on the two cards when they reached seventy-two units. That should have been next year at this time." Conte frowned and scratched his head. "For some reason, the computer went haywire. It started adding everything up as soon as Mr. Kelly pressed the 'activate' button. It just kept adding units until it got to 144, and then it printed Conte Mark onto the graduation list. I just don't understand how . . ."

"I do," said Greg. "You're a lousy computer programmer. Maybe it isn't something you can learn in a single semester."

"I guess not," Conte said. "Still, I did make it do *something*. I mean, it did graduate me. The other problem is, it was supposed to spit out the card for *Mark Conte*, leaving just Conte Mark. It didn't do that either.

The card for *Mark Conte* is still in there, with this year's units recorded on it."

"How do you know?"

"I checked in the print-out ledger."

"Why didn't you just take that card out then?"

"I didn't have time," Conte explained. "Anyhow, I've got another problem."

"What's that?" Greg asked.

"Totals," said Conte.

"Totals?"

"Yup. See, computers are not like people . . ."

"I've noticed."

". . . that is, computers work with total numbers, plus or minus."

"Get to the point," said Greg. "I promised my mother I'd go down to the tide pools with her today."

"The computer," said Conte, "holds a total of 2,117 information cards, one representing each student in the school. Now, this total is recorded in many places. Likewise," Conte said distinctly, "the school population is broken down into four classes. The senior class, for instance, has a total of 653 students."

"So there are 653 names on that graduation list," said Greg.

"Maybe not," Conte explained. "A few student's names might not be on that list. Maybe they didn't complete all their units for some reason, so they won't graduate. That's just it—the computer checks the name and number of each senior against those on the graduation list. If somebody isn't graduating even though he's a senior, his name goes onto a separate list, and the counselors check it out."

Conte gave a deep sigh, then continued. "Pu has me down to graduate, and also as a senior. If I take my name *off* that list, it'll go to the counselor and then—oh boy. I'm wiped out for sure."

"So, what are you going to do?" Greg asked, tapping his fingers impatiently. He still had as many old-man gestures as ever.

"I'm thinking!" Conte shouted. "Listen and try to help. I can't just remove the card for *Mark Conte* either, because then it will change the total freshman enrollment, and Mr. Kelly will know something's wrong. Whenever a kid transfers, Mr. Kelly personally makes the adjustment. And now that the computer's gone on the blink, I don't think he'll let any of us near it . . ."

"What you're telling me," Greg said, "is that you can't take Conte Mark off the list of graduates, and you can't remove *Mark Conte* out of the freshman class—is that right?"

"That's right."

"But you don't want to graduate?"

"That's right."

"Well then," said Greg, "it's obvious."

"What's obvious? Nothing's obvious!"

"Somebody else has to graduate in your place, and you have to stay here."

"As *Mark Conte*?"

"As *Mark Conte*."

"Greg, that's crazy. There is nobody to graduate in my place. Do you want to graduate in my place?"

"Nope. Not me. I'm graduating next year. I couldn't possibly graduate this year. I'm applying for a scholarship in marine biology. It would be too late for this year. Nope. Not me."

"Even if I could get somebody to graduate in my place," Conte argued, "the diploma would have the wrong name on it. It wouldn't work."

Greg pondered for a moment, pacing and smacking his fist into the palm of his hand. "You told me that the computer is mainly concerned with numbers," Greg reminded him. "The numbers are more important than the names, aren't they?"

Conte nodded.

"Wouldn't it be possible just to change the name on that list?" Greg asked. "Couldn't that be done with a typewriter?"

"I guess it could," Conte said slowly. "Actually, there is a typewriter in the computer office that can be used manually—it types exactly the same kinds of letters as the computer. Maybe I could re-type part of the list . . ."

"So all you have to do," said Greg, "is get somebody else to take your place. It should be simple. Lots of guys would love to graduate ahead of time. What about that little guy, Harry Mariot? He's been bored with school for years."

Conte shook his head. "No. It's got to be somebody whose name has the same number of letters as mine. Otherwise it won't work. CONTE MARK." He spelled it out, counting on his fingers. We need somebody with a five letter first name and a four letter last name, or it will mess up the whole sheet. Remember, the computer is oriented toward numbers, and each letter represents a space . . ."

Suddenly Conte stopped. Perhaps the notion had been in back of his mind all along. Perhaps it was a brand new thought. No matter which, he suddenly knew that his idea was the only right one.

Right? No—it was absolutely *superb*. It would get his own name off the graduating list. It would allow him to stay in school, though under the name of *Mark Conte*, but that was a small detail. He'd fix that later. Later, too, he'd redesign his computer program so that next year at this time his plan would function without a hitch. But —one had to be flexible. First things first. And one of the beauties of his present plan was that it would make a story—wow, what a story!—for Charlotta Jones to tell afterward. And he surely needed something with which to induce Charlotta to do him that one last favor.

Not many people realized what was happening at Vista Mar High School on that particular graduation day. To all outward appearances, it was just like any other commencement exercise. The sun shone gently on the students, all scrubbed and gleaming and looking innocent in their gowns and mortar boards. The valedictorian spoke of "this day when we stand on the brink of our adulthood." The honored speaker, Mr. A. Dunlop Peeches, spoke of "these beautiful young people who will carry on our tradition of hard work, service, and integrity."

Mr. Granberg, himself, dignified and handsome in a cap and gown, shook the hand of each graduate as he presented each diploma. His secretary, performing her most cherished duty of the school year, sat at a small table beside Mr. Granberg, reading the name of each graduate into the microphone.

"Abers, Karl. Adams, Felicia. Adsit, Margaret," and so on and on.

As each graduate stepped up to receive the diploma, a ripple of applause came from the audience.

Standing to the side and the rear of the audience,

Conte, Greg, and Pamela watched and listened.

"It's too bad," Greg whispered, "that he can't be here."

"I know," Conte whispered back. "We could have brought him, but it would have been risky."

"I guess it doesn't matter," Pamela whispered. "He'll be glad, anyway."

"Oh, boy, I can't wait!" Conte said, stifling a giggle. "It's going to be unforgettable!" He caught Charlotta's eye and grinned at her. She grinned back from her place among the graduates. Wayne Flint caught Conte's eye and smiled. Having gone straight, he was a little dubious about this plan, but Charlotta had convinced Flint that he need not be involved. Sternly, and with her best interests at heart, Flint had exacted a promise from Charlotta. This was to be her last caper. Positively her last.

Charlotta had given Wayne her solemn promise. Then she and Conte had gone to work on the letter that needed to be written so that the extra diploma could be given to a "close friend of the graduate, as we are going to be *en route* to Paris, and naturally our son will be with us. We regret that he will have to miss the graduation ceremony. Please permit his friend, Kurt Zelinkowitz, to pick up our son's diploma at the graduation exercises. Thank you very much. Sincerely, Georgina Dane."

The letter was received and approved as a matter of course, this being the established procedure when a student couldn't attend graduation. So as not to deplete the ranks, the absentee graduate had to hire a friend to wear his cap and gown, to sit through the ceremony and pick up the diploma and deliver it to the real graduate. This time, of course, the diploma would be delivered to Conte.

It had cost him a mere ten bucks to purchase the services of Kurt Zelinkowitz. The ten bucks were part of Charlotta's payment for the pyramid. With the forty dollars remaining, Conte had settled his account forever with the Comminger Catalogue Company. What a relief to get them off his back!

"Brodski, Stan," droned the secretary. "Brown, Leona. Brunner, Caroline."

Conte smiled to himself. Casually he put his arm around Pamela. Without actually seeming to move, she was suddenly very close to him. Only one thing remained to bother Conte, and while it had upset him considerably a few weeks ago, now it didn't really seem to matter.

"Colbey, Thomas. Conners, Mitzie. Crawley, Hubert. Cummins, Jean."

Two days after Pu had come to a whining halt, Mr. Gordon Kelly had emerged from the computer room. Red-faced, puffing, he was nearly collapsed with fatigue and anger. He assembled the eight students who were privileged to take his special course in computer science. The students gathered around him, waiting silently for the outburst. It never came. Instead, in a sweet and high pitched voice, Mr. Gordon Kelly began.

"Students," he said, "I will show you exactly what it was that did such great harm to our beloved computer. I will show you exactly why your teacher, your computer expert, was forced to spend two entire days going over this machine with a fine-tooth-comb, at great hazard to his health and well-being—I will show you. After I show you," he said tenderly, "you will understand why I shall never again in my career permit any member of the female sex to come anywhere near my computer. You will understand why I shall never again even re-motely consider allowing any person of the female sex to take my course in computer science."

Charlotta, being the only girl in the class, cringed visibly.

Now, from his shirt pocket Mr. Gordon Kelly ex-tracted an object carefully wrapped in a bit of tissue. Slowly, carefully, he unrolled the tissue. Daintily he picked out the object and held it up for the students' inspection. A certain sound—a strangled sort of snort—barely escaped the lips of several of the students, Char-lotta Jones not among them. She alone held her features frozen—frozen into an accusing stare.

Mr. Gordon Kelly, unwilling to accept the obvious, proceeded in this manner: "Miss Jones, kindly tell us, what is the nature of this foreign object that I laboriously removed from the bowels of the computer, and that I now hold in my hand?"

Charlotta Jones said, without blinking an eye, "It's a bobby pin, Mr. Kelly."

"Ah, a bobby pin. And how, Miss Jones, do you suppose such an object would get into the computer room? Do not women customarily wear bobby pins?"

"They do, Mr. Kelly," said Charlotta, "but not me."

For several moments all was silent. Then heatedly Charlotta continued. "I never wore bobby pins in my life! Look at my hair. Do you think I'd ruin my hair with bobby pins?" Furiously she shook her head, and her hair fell over her face and her shoulders. "I never wear bobby pins. Ask anybody! Everybody knows. But I'll tell you who does wear bobby pins. Boys. Three of them in this class. Fred and Paul and Douglas all wear bobby pins. Maybe you can't see them, but I can tell. Look! Just look at their hair," she cried, her face white with fury.

It was true. Fred, Paul, and Douglas, like many of the boys at Vista Mar, wore their hair down beyond their shoulders. Like many, they found that they had to use a bobby pin or two, especially during P.E.

The explosive language that came from the lips of Mr.

Gordon Kelly at this revelation was to remain for decades a part of the lore of Vista Mar High. The story of the bobby pin was repeated whenever anybody asked, "How come Mr. Gordon Kelly won't let anybody into the computer room anymore? How come Mr. Kelly won't teach computer science anymore?"

There ended Conte's plans to mess up the computer, to make it graduate him early. He would just have to go through Vista Mar High like anybody else . . . except, of course, that he was going to be band manager next year. On top of that, he had every intention of becoming student conductor. Since he was going to be spending so much time in the band room, it would certainly be convenient to have a phone in there. He could bring his old-fashioned phone from home. It shouldn't be too hard to hook into the school switchboard—bring the wires up over the roof, through the vents. . . . Come to think of it, it might not be a bad idea to have stereo in there, too. He could tie into the school's PA system . . .

Conte glanced at Pamela. She smiled at him happily. "They're coming to the *D*'s," she said excitedly. "How'd Charlotta ever manage to get it done in *alphabetical order*?"

"Beats me."

The secretary's voice droned on. "Custer, Alice. Dancy, Michael. Dane, Great . . ."

For an instant the faint hum of the microphone itself

could be heard. Then a small twitter rose from one side of the audience. It was quickly covered over by a cough, a loud bout of throat-clearing through the microphone, and the faintly whispered repetition, "Great Dane?"

Up strode Kurt Zelinkowitz, grinning like a pumpkin, his amber eyes squeezed into mere slits. A small ripple of applause came from some of the graduates. In a moment it was over. All was sober decorum. Few people realized that on this day the principal of Vista Mar High School had approved and presented a graduation diploma to a Great Dane dog.

Thus, while it was inconspicuous, the Mark of Conte *was* left, at least in the hearts and minds of some. Those who knew of the prank truly appreciated the wit, the flair, the *savoir-faire* of it all.

Conte's mother, when told the whole story, laughed until she cried, then hugged Conte and warned him most severely never, never to do such a thing again.

His father nodded, roared, hollered, and grunted, "All's well that ends well, son. Be flexible."

Pamela gave Conte a shy and tender kiss and said, "You're a genius, Conte. Let's go down to Katz Beach."

And Dag—old Dag—seemed to know that now, after so many years of frustration, he was really OK. Yeah, he was an OK dog, with a high school diploma (which is better than a common old pedigree), a *high school diploma* to prove it. He found himself a little Labrador a block away, named Lenny, and told that conceited little poodle exactly what she could do with her pedigree! Yessir!

All that summer—that long and lovely summer—Pamela and Conte went down to Katz Beach nearly every day. They relaxed and rode the surf and laughed and drank strawberry sodas, and Conte began to make a few plans. Oh, he'd probably go to summer school next summer, take some extra courses and graduate a year early. Then he'd go off to Chicago, most likely, and become an inventor.

Meanwhile, there were a few matters to tend to right here in Vista Mar.

For example, somebody had to defeat A. Dunlop Peeches in the next school board election. Someone. Hmm. Someone who was the wife of a psychologist, a prize-winning artist, and who had a son who would gladly serve as campaign manager. It shouldn't be too hard. You can do just about anything, once you get familiar with a town, learn the ropes, know your way around . . . and when you have a few friends.